MW01600231

"Do Something!"

A Collection of Short Stories, Opinions, Articles, and Excerpts

by
Robert A. Johnson

As we grow older our lives seem to come together like a lengthy story where all characters meet, where hopes and dreams become real, where twists and turns unwind, where purpose is revealed.

ISBN: 9781073744183

PRINTED IN THE USA
by Kindle

1

Contents

———————————

A Father and His Sons

Over dinner our father recalled one of his favorite stories. Dad was always ready to tell a joke, relay a story, or have fun with us kids. But as I said before, he was a hard worker, an independent man, and a true entrepreneur at heart. He was forever coming up with some crazy ideas to try to earn a better living. I think he could best be characterized as a cross between three well-known people we all have learned to love.

Dad was exactly like the opinionated television hard-headed Archie Bunker of *All In The Family* who was always giving his wife, poor ding bat Edith, a difficult time. Our father was also the spitting image of the lovable, rotund Ralph Kramden—the endearing Mr. Jackie Gleason of *The Honeymooners* who would every time foul up his scheming attempts to start a hair-brained business and ultimately end up kissing his steadfast wife Alice, saying "Baby, you're the greatest!"

And of course, there is no doubt, my dad Johnny Johnson was like the jolly cartoon character of Fred Flintstone in Bedrock who mirrored the antics of Kramden in a much earlier time. That was our dear old Dad all rolled into one. How could you not love him?

One spring day when both my brother Eddie and I were in the military away from home, Dad had decided to set up a fruit and vegetable stand at a dirt clearing along the narrow main street near his house. He knew where to buy the produce wholesale in the city and for some reason thought he could make his new venture work. This from a man who couldn't even find his way around our small kitchen at Dewey Ave without Mom's help.

We had heard this story told numerous times on the front porch, but he often continued his tale. Dad had everything planned out. But there was one problem. He needed to obtain a permit from the town to set up his new business. So Dad went down to the small Wilmington police station to fill out the necessary forms. The old police chief, Harold 'Slugger' Reed, an ex-baseball player who prided himself in knowing everything that went on in his town, reviewed Dad's application and frowned.

The big country boy said to Dad, "Why should I approve this? I don't know you. I've never even heard of you." He was ready to dismiss Dad's hopes of having a simple neighborhood roadside fruit stand business.

Dad, who lived by the principles he grew up with and instilled into his offspring, stood tall and looked straight into the chief's eyes, two bulls in a standoff, and said, "Why should you approve it? Well, I've lived in this town for over fifteen years and I've raised four sons here. And now you tell me you've never heard of me."

He paused. "That's why you should give me the permit."

The chief stared at Dad for the longest time, then smirked. Without saying another word he nodded, signed the papers and handed them to Dad.

And that, my friends, I'm happy to say, is what the Johnson boys grew up with.

Excerpt from the author's book, *Looking For Eddie*

Fallen Hero

Eddie was a friendly, shy boy who grew up in Wilmington, a small country town north of Boston. His Dad had decided he wanted his boys to live a better life away from the dirty tenements in the city. Trees, fresh air, a lake to swim in, a place to fish, room for young kids to run free. As for many families of those times it was a new beginning.

Eddie and his brothers learned the basics of New England life in that cottage town. Follow the 'Golden Rule' and be kind to others. Believe in God and do what is right. Work hard for what you want and help others along the way. Serve your country because you are fortunate enough to be born here.

And above all, be happy.

The teenage girls loved Eddie because of his quiet demeanor and gorgeous wavy hair. He was a smart kid, but never at the top of his class. He was a good boy, but was known to skip church services or high school classes from time to time. He really never got in trouble except for maybe driving too fast in his first car. He was a typical American youngster with his entire promising life ahead of him.

As a senior he had had enough of school, and like many young men, he had joined the U.S. Army. Unfortunately, the Vietnam War thousands of miles away was still raging on and more soldiers were needed to protect our freedom and to stop the spread of Communism. That's what Eddie believed and so he went where he was needed.

He was a radio man with his small unit immersed in the jungles of Southeast Asia. His brother once asked him, after Eddie had returned home, "What was it like in Vietnam?" Even more reserved than before, Eddie had hesitantly answered, "We lived in the mud and slept under culvert pipes cut length wise. They were covered with sand bags to protect us from mortar fire." That was all he ever said about his experience in the foreign jungle.

War changes people and Eddie was no exception.

Years later, after a long period of being 'lost' to his family, Eddie was found. But it wasn't a good thing. He was in the ICU at the Las Vegas Sunrise Hospital, lost in a coma. Doctors showed his family the MRI images of an aggressive brain tumor ever expanding, robbing Eddie of what was the rest of his life. Some believed the tumor was caused by the toxic Agent Orange heavily sprayed during the Asian war. Perhaps. Perhaps not.

At the young age of fifty-five Eddie passed away.

Eddie loved his Boston sports teams. Red Sox. Bruins. Celtics. Every morning he would read only the sports sections of the newspaper, checking scores, following favorite players, anticipating upcoming games. Because of his growing tumor his eyesight quickly faded until he became completely blind. When bad things happen often good things take their place. His girlfriend Sammy, strangely enough a sweet lady from Southeast Asia, would read the sports pages to Eddie up until the end.

Eddie never invented anything. He never cured horrible diseases. He never wrote provoking books. He never really found the freedom that he once fought for. He was just a regular guy. A good boy. A good son. A good friend. A good soldier. And he was a good brother to me who I will forever miss.

Edward T. Johnson, CPL USA Vietnam
1951-2006

Man on a Park Bench

Joe Higgins decided to walk home from work after a long day at his office. He usually took bus number nine, a quick fifteen minute ride down Main Street to his apartment. But today was such a nice day. It was a half hour stroll through the small grassy park in the center of town. The late spring sun was warm and comfortable, heating the earth, reviving the maple trees, the thick rye grass. The sky was clear and pale blue with little chance of rain.

It was one of those days when simply being outside felt good.

People were in the park. Afternoon joggers dressed in running gear and high-priced sneakers attempting to stay fit. Lean, slim, and glistening with exertion. Teenagers tossed a baseball back and forth breaking in new leather gloves, loosening up and hoping for a winning baseball season. Adults were walking their dogs, enjoying the outdoors before dinner time. On a bench along the road was an old man feeding the birds.

Picture perfect.

Carrying a light jacket slung over his shoulder Joe slowly walked the edge of the park, his feet sinking inches into the thick carpet-like grass. He moved toward the bench. It faced inward offering a great view of the pleasant activities. The old man acknowledged the office worker as he approached. It was a gentle nod, a friendly welcome from one stranger to another.

"Good afternoon," Joe said. "Okay if I share your bench?"

The old man moved to the left of the seat leaving ample room. "Most certainly," he responded.

Joe sat on the seat, draping his jacket over the side arm. The warmth of the metal bench seeped into his back instantly relaxing him. The old man had a clear plastic bag of what appeared to be puffed rice. He was tossing small handfuls for the birds. He noticed Joe looking at the bag. "Rice cakes," the old man said. "I'm not very fond of them. Too dry and tasteless."

"Diet food," Joe joked.

Birds flocked to the crumbled grains of rice. Sparrows and wrens. Robins and blue jays. And of course, city pigeons. They came right up to the old man, even to his outreached hand as he offered the free meal. They seemed unafraid. Some of the birds hopped onto the old man's legs and arms waiting for food as if they were on a tree branch with no hint of being harmed.

Two brown squirrels came forward and boldly climbed onto the old man's lap. He gave chunks of dried rice to the animals. They took them in their hands and chewed without moving away. The old man stroked their bushy tails as they sat quietly, completely at ease with the human. Joe had never witnessed such a gentle, trusting bond with animals.

A young lady with her daughter walked on the sidewalk in front of the bench. Her baby was a beautiful child, perhaps three years old. She wore a yellow summer dress and cute shiny black shoes. Her dark bright eyes displayed pure youthful innocence. The girl stopped her mother and approached the old man on the bench. She went to him as if invited. Like she was going to see her grandfather. She smiled and hugged the gentleman.

He said something to her in a foreign language Joe didn't understand. Then he tenderly caressed the young girl's head and kissed her on her forehead, speaking to her again in unfamiliar words. The girl backed off a bit, nodded a couple of times, smiled innocently, then returned to her

Korean mom. She turned and waved goodbye to the old man as they continued their walk.

Joe stared at the man beside him. He seemed an unusual gentleman. He may have been eighty or even ninety years old. His white-gray hair was a bit long, but not shaggy. It was blown back as if he had just gotten off a motorcycle. But there was no motorcycle in sight. His face was tanned and exhibited generous wrinkles. His clothes were worn but clean. A white shirt, a buttoned-up long sleeve brown sweater, dark pants, and scuffed brown, laced shoes.

The old man could have escaped from a senior care home, longing for brief freedom outside where the world lived. Or he may simply have been a retired gentleman out for his daily walk interacting with younger people, his elderly wife or responsible children waiting for his return. Either way, to Joe he appeared to be quite alert, his faculties in proper order. His bag of rice was empty now and the birds and squirrels had gone.

A Frisbee dropped several feet in front of the park bench. A large German Shepard ran, trying to retrieve it. Seeing the old man, the dog stopped. It went to the strange gentleman and lowered its head onto his lap, his big dog eyes looking up at the man. The man rubbed the animal's head, behind its ears, under its chin. He patted the dog like they were old friends, long time companions almost. Then the dog backed off and picked up the Frisbee with its teeth, and returned to the boy throwing it.

"You have lots of friends here, don't you?" Joe couldn't help but ask.

The old man grinned. "I like animals. They don't judge. They just are."

Joe liked that. It made him think. "I had a dog when I was young," he commented. "He was a great dog, full of energy, fun to be with. We played right here in this park a long time ago."

The old man nodded. "Yes, Sam was a beautiful animal."

Joe paused a moment. "How do you know my dog's name?" he asked, bewildered and mystified.

"I know things," the old man explained. "And I remember everything."

"So you have been coming here, to this bench for a long time?"

"I sit on a lot of benches. Benches are everywhere."

The old man leaned down from his seat to pick up a green maple leaf blown toward the bench. He held it up to the diminishing sunlight. Turned it over and marveled at it. "Quite a design. Perfect symmetry, every part of it, every cell having its purpose. And to think there are billions of them, no two alike, none identical. Each one different and unique, like snowflakes. Truly a wonder."

Joe looked at the leaf, then at the old man. "Are you an artist or something?"

"I suppose you could say that."

"What's your field? Painting, sculpture, music, literature?" Joe inquired of this intriguing stranger.

"I like to dabble in them all. Keeps me young, though it doesn't show. Some people say I should stop, as if it doesn't matter any longer. Few people really care about my work now."

"You should never stop doing what you love to do," Joe remarked.

"I don't plan on it. But to tell you the truth, fewer and fewer people are interested in my art these days."

Joe glanced at his watch. It was time for him to go. His wife would be cooking dinner and expecting him soon.

"I should be heading out now," Joe addressed the old man. "It was a pleasure talking with you. You, my friend, are an interesting person."

"And you as well, my dear man."

Joe rose from the bench and began walking away. The old man called out to him, "Joe, you have a very good day tomorrow and a wonderful life."

Joe raised his hand as if to wave, but then stopped. "How do you know my name?" he asked the old man as he turned.

But the old man was gone.

Joe looked to the right. Then he looked to the left. The old man was well on his way down the sidewalk. He was holding the hand of the small child he had spoken to minutes earlier. Joe shook his head. Then he saw the old man on the far side of the park sitting on the grass and patting another dog. He closed his eyes for a second. He was tired. Long day. Crossing the street he saw the old man looking in the front window of a bakery. Two young boys at his side were pointing at the delicious display of cookies and colorful cupcakes.

Joe walked home confused at what he had seen, puzzled by the thoughts running through his mind. He unlocked the door and entered his home. His wife heard him and called out, "Hello Joe. How was your day?"

But Joe didn't answer. Instead of going straight to the kitchen he went into the den without saying a word.

He sat on his favorite chair, the comfortable stuffed one facing the television. His wife found him. "I thought I heard you," she said.

Joe just sat there. Silent. Staring nowhere, but with a strange grin on his face.

"Did you hear anything about that promotion?" his wife asked.

"Ah...no. Not today. They said a decision would be made tomorrow."

"Are you okay, Joe?" she asked.

"Yes."

"You look...I don't know. Different."

"Honey...I think I saw God today."

Hot Dogs, Beans, and Brown Bread

We were having a small BBQ on our back patio here in Arizona. It was a nice sunny day. Not too hot, but perfect for eating outside. My wife brought out an old plate from my childhood days in Wilmington. It was oval and solid and made from bone China. Small chips and scratches attested to its many years of use.

It was my beloved hot dogs and Boston baked beans plate from the mid-1950s. Every Saturday for as long as I can remember, it was standard issue for one of my favorite kid meals. Of course there was always a side order of warmed brown bread with raisins from a can. People out here in the desert think bread in a can is crazy.

What do they know? They don't know what they're missing.

Anyway, the old plate reminded me of our family weekly meals way back in the day and how it seemed most every family around ate the same foods on the same days. Like an unspoken, unwritten tradition.

Sundays were always large suppers of juicy meatloaf or spaghetti and meatballs and fresh baked rolls with a full house of family and friends.

Mondays were leftovers. Day old meatloaf always tasted better the day after.

Tuesdays we may have had creamed peas on toast (we really didn't have a lot of money.)

Wednesdays, of course, were Prince Spaghetti days, which was common in those days since the Prince Spaghetti factory was nearby.

Thursdays were anything-goes days. Could be cold cereal or fried bologna sandwiches.

Fridays had to be fish days since most of us were Catholic and it was a sin to eat meat.

Saturdays we were back to the boiled hot dogs, beans, and brown bread.

Simple long time memories that stick with me.

I'm keeping this plate.

From a Sept. 2018 author's conversation posted on the site

'I'm Lucky—I grew up in Wilmington'

Shopping Hell

While my dear wife was away enjoying her vacation I was stuck home all alone. Being a temporary bachelor, I planned on buying beer and pre-cooked chicken for dinner. Easy peasy. Unfortunately, it was a Wednesday and I found myself trapped in the grocery store to hell on senior discount day.

There was a long line near the liquor department.

The longest line I'd seen all day.

A man dressed in a cheap tuxedo was passing out small plastic cups of wine samples. Zinfandels, merlots, house brands. The really cheap stuff. But the shoppers didn't care. Free wine and cheese at the Safeway.

Happy Hour was never so good for these over the hill free-loaders.

Two electric go-carts had crashed into each other. That's how these people drive their Buicks too. One was flipped over with its driver screaming on the floor, "I was here first. You cut in line." She was desperately pressing her alert button hanging from her neck. "Help me! Help me!" The other was waiting for another cup of vino, oblivious to the 'grandma down' emergency call.

A couple of wine drinking patrons were curled up and sleeping on the floor. One guy who must have gone for several refills was acting silly and telling off-colored jokes. "There once was a man from Nantucket..." Another was one of those angry drunks stomping his feet and yelling, "Hey, where are the damn stewardesses?"

I pushed a few tipsy cane carriers over as I got closer to the cold beer. It was like tipping cows in the field while they slept standing upright. As the drunkards fell onto their bony asses a loud chorus of laughter from their friends filled the store.

It was a mean spirited crowd.

With two cases of cold beer safely in my shopping cart I was ready to go.

Oh!

Almost forgot my fried chicken to go.

I went the long way through the store, bypassing the thinning buffet crowds. When I returned to the deli I looked at the number on the lit-up sign.

Someone yelled out, "Number 73?...73?"

WTF?

How in the hell did they go through all those numbers in such a short time?

"Hey!" I shrieked, holding up my ticket. "I'm number seventy-two."

"Sorry sir, you weren't here. I'm serving seventy-three now. You can take another ticket if you'd like."

You think the clerk cared?

She didn't care.

She just wanted to get done with this fuckin' Wednesday crowd. To tell you the truth, I couldn't blame her.

I should have fought her. I should have complained to someone, the manager, anyone. But they were all in the wine line.

Fuck it!

I was too tired to pursue my rights as a properly numbered shopper. Instead of causing a scene I simply walked over to the ticket wheel. I looked around at the zombies waiting their turn.

So I took my new number.

Then I took another.

And I continued taking them until it had reached five hundred. I had enough numbers to shop here for the rest of my friggin' life, but you know damn well I was never coming back here again. I tossed the rolled up tickets in my cart and went to the hot chicken section. I walked around to the back of the counter, grabbed my bag of heated chicken parts and went on my way.

Let's see how long these people wait for service now.

I had everything I really needed and went out front to the checkout counter.

Ba-dum...ba-dum. The defective cart's wheels were getting worse.

OMG!

Now what?

The entire front of the store was full of old people.

Every cashier was open. All twenty of them!

The lines stretched back into the food aisles.

People were leaning on each other. Walkers were entangled. Oxygen lines were unplugged just to get closer to the checkout. Abandoned electric wheelies blocked some lanes, testament that some of the seniors were faking it just to get around the easy way.

Just as I'd always suspected.

I found a line that extended into the candy section. Some of the customers were nibbling on candy bars from the 'open' bags. One gently retired woman was going up and down the line passing out Reese's Pieces to the patrons like it was Halloween. It was party time for the clueless seniors who were out for a good time before being dragged back to their cubed cages at the old peoples' centers.

My bag of hot chicken smelled good and I almost peeled the taped price tag off to take a few bites. But in this crowd of scavengers that would have been a huge mistake.

I would have been bludgeoned for a simple drumstick. Clobbered for a deep fried wing. Raped and pillaged for a golden brown breast.

Well…probably not raped.

The savages were uncivilized, drunk on the free wine, satiated on the free goodies, delirious with their sugar rush. It was ten times worse than my imaginary flings with the strippers and wild rock bands.

And the blue hairs loved it.

The line barely moved.

I was getting older by the inch. I heard strange sounds in front and behind me. Then from a line or two over. In minutes it was resonating from every corner of the store. The old people had eaten.

Their systems were primed.

Their hearing depleted.

Yes, the air was awash with air biscuits.

They puffed all around me. Pinned me to the shelving. Slammed me into my cart. My hands tensed on the handle, my eyes watered from the fog, my nose deadened by the odorous smells. I was captive in the humanity of old farts.

These people would put my Uncle Joe to shame, which if you ever spent any time with my Uncle Joe after a meal, was no easy task. I had been warned about this phenomenon a long time ago by my dear departed grandfather.

I needed a drink and looked down at the cases of beer in my cart. No, a shot of whiskey would be better.

Maybe a hit of cocaine to dull the senses.

I was surrounded by these…these old people tooting up a storm. A few single notes here, some doubles and triples there. A staccato of machine gun-like musical tunes. By golly, the music was that of a brass ass orchestra.

I needed to get out.

Please God, I'll leave the beer if you show me the way. But the noise was too loud even for Him to hear my pleas.

Doctor Kevorkian, help me!

But I was left alone without help.

My line was slowly getting shorter. People were shuffling out of the store. Some were being pushed to their appropriate senior buses. Others lingered back waiting for their slower friends.

I mean the really slow ones.

The store gradually emptied as the cashiers did their job. I was getting excited. I was almost next to being checked out.

Ba-dum...ba-dum.

I moved up a few paces.

By now my beer was warm and my chicken was cold. I was beyond pissed off. I was...beside myself, and if it wasn't for the simple fact that I was so close to the cashier's conveyor belt, I was on the verge of going postal.

Instead, I remained calm and set my eyes on the goal post.

Ba-dum...ba-dum.

Finally, the old bag in front of me moved up to pay for her shit. She got a leg on her tennis ball walker tangled up with one of her knotted feet. In agony I watched her pull loose.

Almost there Bob, stay composed.

Keep thinking, 'It's only a dream.'

But it wasn't.

I began biting my tongue and turning redder than a pissed on hydrant.

The nice senior citizen lady in front of me unloaded her crap from the wire basket attached to her walker. I couldn't believe what I was seeing.

Two things?!

She had two items!

She had to have been in the store for close to four friggin' hours and she only bought two fuckin' things?! What the hell did she come here for?

To eat?

To drink?

Play cards?

Fill out the sewing club?

Aggravate the shit out of me?

Who the hell are these sadistic people anyway?

I knew what was about to happen next.

Don't ask me how, but I just knew it.

Hope for the best and expect the worst.

Right?

Isn't that some sort of old boy scout saying?

The store must have carried over twenty thousand products. Maybe more. And my nemesis in front of me had only two of them.

Yup!

You guessed it.

Her Jelly Bellies were quickly scanned. But her denture cream wouldn't beep.

WTF!

These words will be imbedded in my brain for as long as I live, maybe longer.

"Price check," the cashier called out over the intercom.

I dropped my head into my hands and thought about tearing it off and ending this ordeal. But I was so close. Five minutes and thirty two seconds later a bag boy showed up with the price.

Now, you might think I'm making this stuff up.

Right?

No.

You can't make up this kind of shit.

Keep reading. It's too surreal.

The cashier rang up the denture cream.

"That's $3.49 ma'am."

The grandmotherly woman looked at the cashier and said, "Oh dear, that's too much. I'll have to put it back and only buy the candy."

If there is truly a hell, I was stuck in it with no way out.

I wanted to say, 'Listen you miserable hag, I've been standing in this fuckin' line for over an hour. You buy two god-damned things, one of which doesn't have a friggin' price. Then you say it's too expensive. You either buy the fuckin' tooth glue or I'll knock those damn ceramics right out of your mouth.'

But I didn't say a thing.

I just smiled through my raging anger, a defeated man trying to get a few groceries while his wife was gone enjoying her life. The old broad finally paid for her one item and wobbled out of my way.

I was finally face to face with the cashier.

Eureka!

I felt like I had just won the lottery.

I could almost feel the winds of freedom on my stressed out face. Home was so near I could almost smell the hotdogs.

The cashier scanned my shit, then asked me, "Senior?"

"Not when I first came here, but now, yes," I answered.

"I mean are you a senior over sixty-five? Today is our Senior Wednesday Discount Day."

No shit!

"No, I'm not sixty-five yet. I feel like a hundred and five to tell you the truth."

"Well," the lady said, "discounts are only for people over..."

"Yeah, yeah. I know. Forget it," I said.

She saw the despair in my eyes, the desperation in my face, the defeat in my body language. "Since you waited in line so long I'll give you the discount anyway."

"Why, thank you."

"Except on the beer," she added.

"Of course."

I paid for my stuff and saved a whole dollar and ninety-six cents, which meant my time in this hell hole was worth a whopping forty-nine cents an hour.

To further aggravate me the punk bag boy put each of my items in separate plastic bags.

"Have a nice day sir," he said.

"Too late for that," I remarked on my way out.

"Too damn late for that."

Ba-dum...ba-dum.

Excerpt from the author's book *Pleasure Trip*

Let Them Learn

Some months ago I spent an entire day at a local junior high school as a guest speaker. It was the first time I'd been in public school since dirt was invented.

It reminded me how absolutely terrible our education really is.

A seventh grade English teacher who had attended one of my goal setting seminars had invited me. She asked if I would be willing to give a brief presentation on basic writing skills. At the time her classes were working on writing their short stories.

"Of course," I agreed.

What possibly could go wrong?

I thought it would be enjoyable. Maybe even enlightening. Perhaps I could share the complexities of the writing process, the importance of written communication. I might even be able to inspire the students.

So I put together a short visual presentation sprinkled with some juvenile photos to capture the students' attention. I also brought along several of my novels as examples of creative writing.

I figured we could review and talk about the basic components of the written language such as book titles, topic sentences, character development, plot advancement, internal conflicts, purpose of the story, etc.

Upon entering the classroom I felt as if I had returned to my pre-JFK school room. Rows of old desks with attached seats and lift-up tops lined the room in straight lines, front to back. The walls were stark. Barren of any school work. No posters. No colorful projects. No personal achievements for all to see.

Just a large clock ticking loudly, clicking away the seconds.

Stacks of boxes and piles of worn textbooks filled the rear corners. The teacher's desk to the side was littered with books and folders and papers and reports. Clearly she was overwhelmed. I immediately remembered why I hated school. I stood at the front whiteboard searching for a small section to write on.

When the first bell of the day rang, the kids hurried into the room and dropped their loaded backpacks beneath their desks. They pulled out their notebooks and pencils, eyeballing the old guy out front. They sat quietly in their seats waiting for instruction.

I've always believed that structure is good. Organization and neatness and preparation are great, essential really, but this place was a true institution.

Where was the stimulation? I thought.

The excitement to learn?

The creative environment?

The spirit to discover?

It wasn't there.

Let me first say the teacher was a great instructor and came highly recommended. But it seemed she was bogged down in bureaucratic mandates, numerous internal and state reports, and frankly, outdated, inefficient standards and methods of teaching.

Of course all of this is my mere opinion.

Classes were fifty minutes short. Students were rushed all day long from room to room, from one subject to another. They did what they could do in the time allowed and then shuffled off to the next place on their schedules. As an outsider, learning, true learning, appeared to be an afterthought.

Knowing the students were being forced to complete their writing assignments, I asked this one question: "Who is excited about writing their story?" The classroom was quiet. Of the twenty-five students only three raised their hands. I turned and wrote the numbers 3/25 on the whiteboard.

Enthusiasm had been successfully purged from the classroom.

Something was definitely wrong!

I asked a series of questions of the students. "What do you like?" "What do you dream about?" "What do you want to be or do in your future?"

All fair questions, I thought for twelve and thirteen year olds. The floodgates opened up. Hands from every row were raised, even from the back seats. This stranger in front of them wanted to know more about them. What they thought. What they felt. What they wanted. He wanted to hear their voices. He was genuinely interested in what they had to say, what they wanted to share.

We discussed books and movies, and how they related to life. The students asked questions about my books and thought-provoking titles. The who and the why and the how.

They showed interest.

They wanted to learn.

They told of their inner stories. They shared their secret dreams. They openly talked about what they liked to read and how they would do things differently. They had someone to listen to them.

It was a good and interesting class. They were great kids. Near the end of the class I wasn't as depressed as I had first been. My final question was, again: "Who is excited about writing their story?"

Hands went up. Almost all of them. I counted and turned to the whiteboard. New score: 19/25.

And so the day went on.

Four more classes.

Nearly a hundred and thirty young, impressionable, eager students wanting to learn.

3/22 became 18/22.

2/23 turned into 14/23.

7/28 grew to 25/28.

1/29 rose to 17/29.

Of course I would be foolish to expect all hands to be raised. But, the point is that all learners, from young children to adults, want to achieve the excitement of learning and trying new things.

As educators and mentors, it's up to us to encourage them.

It's up to us to let them learn.

From a May 2017 Linked-in post by author.

High School Reunion

It was not too long ago I joined a terrific group of people, though I'm really not a joiner. I like to do my own thing in my own time and at my own pace. That's probably why I've been self-employed most of my life. Self-unemployed on occasion too. But basically I consider myself very lucky. Good things happen to me almost on a daily basis.

I found this group, a community really, called 'I'm Lucky—I grew up in Wilmington.' It made me smile and laugh and reminisce and appreciate years long past and friendships long faded. Life moves quickly, but memories remain forever. This group of great people from a great place during a great time has renewed and brightened many terrific moments of my youth. I've been flooded with visions of those days.

Buying a two-scoop ice cream cone from the best store in the world, Tat's, in the summer with beach sand dragged in from the lake across the street. Five cents baseball card packs with a slab of sweat smelling bubble gum. Trading in empty soda (tonic) bottles found along the road and in the creek for two pennies each. Spending my meager ten cents weekly allowance on Superman comic books and penny candy.

Mildred H. Rogers four-room elementary school house next to Town Beach where I embarrassed myself by misspelling the word 'am' in a spelling contest. The round Glen Road School that had the greatest teachers. Wilmington High School where a shy, unsure, pimpled face kid had a difficult time. The tiny library across the street that had all the books in the world. Steven's Market and DeMoulas Grocery and Friendlies' Ice Cream and Scottie's Donuts.

Playing with childhood friends in the back woods. Swinging on Tarzan ropes. Hiding in the thicket. Fishing for perch and bluegills at Silver Lake. Staying out 'til dark with no concern of being hurt—or worse. Running a go-cart built from discarded boards and bent nails down the hill with no brakes.

Five person baseball games in someone's backyard, peppered with arguments and fights. Snowball fights from hand-built snow forts with neighboring kids. Playing Army with sticks and Pirates with inner tubes and Treasure Hunters in the forest and swamp. Ice skating on thin cracking ice and fighting off wasp nest with willow branches and scooping for polliwogs and chasing garden snakes.

Eating supper with the whole family. Sundays meant a large meal. Mondays were leftovers. Tuesdays, creamed peas on toast. Wednesday of course was spaghetti day. Thursday was open, Fridays fish, Saturdays had to be franks and beans with canned brown bread!

Watching TV in black and white, only three stations, and the programming ending its broadcasts at 11:00 PM with the American flag and our National Anthem. Reciting the Pledge of Allegiance every day in school and offering a moment of silence to give thanks.

Old friends like Bill and John and Charles and Jeanne and Leslie and Jack and Dave and Hank and Danny and Ralphy and Diane and Freddy and many others.

That was our universe.

And then we went our own ways.

Moved out, moved on, and moved up. We grew up and suddenly turned around to find ourselves where we are some fifty years later. We were most definitely lucky to grow up in Wilmington in those simpler days. Much like George Bailey in the movie had discovered, it truly has been a wonderful life.

May every one of my old and renewed friends from Wilmington enjoy your time together at the reunion. May each and every one of you be well and be kind.

From the author's post in
'I'm Lucky—I grew up in Wilmington' site.

Letter to My New Great-Grandson

To: Owen James Oliver
Date: August 28, 2018

Things Learned in Life...

Today is a very good day.

You came into this world today.

You were born to awesome parents.

You are loved beyond belief by so many people.

And most of us haven't even met you yet.

Here are some things we learned in life.

> **BE KIND**. It will surround you and follow you forever.

> **BE STRONG**. When things go wrong, fix them and move on.

> **BE HUMBLE**. Great things you do will be known and come back to you.

> **BE PATIENT**. Good things will come in time.

BE GOOD. There is not enough goodness in
the world. Change that.

BE GRATEFUL. God is on your side.
Always believe.

BE HAPPY. Your joy will infect others in
countless ways.

BE LOVED. Love is amazing. Share it with
abundance.

My dear great-grandson Owen, follow these lessons and
you will have a wonderful life. If you don't, I will come
back and kick your ass!

With boundless love, Great-grandma and Great-grandpa
Johnson

OUR STORIES
by The Dreamers

As an English Language Acquisition instructor for the Department of Adult Education at Cochise Community College my foreign adult students and I were invited to the college executive board meeting on April 12, 2016 to share a special project my students had finished.

I had an opportunity to read this letter to members of the board.

'With us tonight are some amazing people. Some come from very difficult times, sad, often frightening situations. Some are well educated while others are not. Some came here to their new country uncertain about the unexpected, but excited for the possibilities.

'They are hard workers. Some work every day of the week, some twelve hour shifts, some have two or three jobs at a time. They never complain. They just do their work and look toward a better future. They recognize the opportunities available to them and they appreciate support offered them.

'They are America's new immigrants and they come to school every day with a smile, ready to improve their English skills and their places in their new country.

'They are my terrific students in our Career-Infused ELA classes. My name is Bob Johnson and I am proud to be their teacher.

'Like every one of us, they too have dreams and goals. Some small, some big. From obtaining a driver's license to becoming an American citizen. From getting a job to starting their own business. From saving money to buying a car or a house. Our students know that dreams do come true through hard work, persistence, determination, and self-confidence. It's our job as teachers to help them succeed.

'A few months ago my students were asked, as a typical assignment, to write a short story about their lives. Nothing elaborate, just a few pages. They weren't very thrilled about the long homework required to complete the project. So I sweetened the deal. 'What if everyone wrote their story and we put them together in book form and have them published?' I suggested.

'Instantly, everyone was onboard. It was an experiment in goal setting, the foundation of our classes. Task, hard work, deadline, all of which we focus on in school.

'Now, to write, edit (several times), proof, format, print, and deliver such a book in less than six weeks seemed an impossible project. But it was important to the students. This was the first time in their lives they were asked to share what they had gone through to come to America. It was their first time they actually had a voice that people would hear. Everyone deserves to be heard. Everyone has a story to tell.

'Two days prior to the deadline their books were delivered to class. Without doubt it was one of the most impressive accomplishments in their lives. They were excited and proud, as they should be, for what they had completed as student-authors.

'As a gift of appreciation, members of the board, please accept signed copies of my students' book, *OUR STORIES* by The Dream Makers.'

Cochise College President J.D. Rottweiller, Ph.D. wrote an inspiring article about my students and their achievements in the college's magazine.

Change is Good

I was about to have some fun. I was going to be someone other than myself. I could be anyone I wanted to be. With a quick snap of my fingers I could instantly and magically become someone else.

I could turn into a person I never met before. He could be real or just a figment of my whacked out imagination. Old Bob Swift could be rich or famous, preferably both, if I had my druthers. He could be ivy-league educated or royally refined. He could be adorably charming or statesman-like charismatic.

Anything I'm not, I could become.

I could be a man I might like to be in an alternative world, if such things were possible. Like in Rod Serling's *Twilight Zone*, I could be the alter ego of myself from a faraway planet. A reversed or mirrored image, whatever I choose. A clone of someone remarkably heroic or devilishly evil.

I could be someone I would enjoy having a friendly conversation with and maybe shoot the breeze over a couple of cold ones. I could talk about pressing worldly issues, high finance mergers and acquisitions, theories concerning the universe.

These things and more are possible if one can only dream and believe in them.

Let me show you how.

Snap!

The old boring couch potato, senior desk jockey nearing a formidable retirement from some obscure business suddenly vanished. Banished to his safe, steady, and predictable existence. Relegated to his four hours of watching idiotic television every evening. Left alone with nothing but his remote control. Sent back to his lackluster life where nothing really happens and even less matters.

Poof!

Viola!

A new me showed up in his place!

It was deliciously naughty and hellishly exhilarating.

Hey, come on!

Don't tell me the same feeling has never crossed your mind. Haven't you ever thought about being someone else? Putting on a mask? Hiding behind a new persona? Messing with strangers?

You're a damn liar if you tell me you haven't.

Haven't you ever wished you could be that cool guy in school that everyone liked? Or didn't you ever want to be the popular jock that all the girls were dying to date? Or perhaps it would be nice to be the tall, dark handsome celebrity surrounded by millions of fans.

Wouldn't it be great for a change to be the rich guy who could afford all the luxuries and fantasies imaginable, spread the wealth amongst your loved ones and friends, enjoying life to the max?

What would it be like if for once you were the life of the party, the comic who could bring an audience to tears, the author whose words inspired, the prophet revealing the secret of life?

How would it feel if you were the hero in the crowd, the leader of the silent and meek, the benefactor of the oppressed? Wouldn't it be terrific if you could fix all the wrongs, or create fantastic time-saving devices, or invent the next super fuel, or discover sought-after cures?

Damn straight it would!

Excerpt from author's book, *Last Bus to Korat*

In The Beginning...

"Gentlemen," the bellowing voice cut through the quarrelsome clamor in the grand meeting hall. Silence blanketed the room with due respect for the eloquent speaker. The man slowly gazed into the eyes of his fellow countrymen.

"We are living in a time of difficult and dangerous decisions." The room full of statesmen and attorneys and merchants and land owners gave their full attention to the distinguished leader. It was time for words to give way to action.

"What man amongst us dares to stand strong against the evil that suppresses us? Who is willing to sacrifice all that he has for his sons and daughters, his future generations, his fellow citizens? Is there a soul here today who is prepared to risk all his worldly goods, his reputation, even his God given life, in order to right the wrongs he has so long suffered? Who is willing to come forth to speak his mind against overwhelming adversity, to denounce tyranny, to let it be known to the world that he shall fight to the very end to preserve the divine human desire to be unshackled as a truly free man? What man before me pledges his word and his bond toward the independence of a new found sovereign nation dedicated to the needs and wants of its own populace? Is not human liberty a natural right, deserving of every man's effort to preserve?"

Cheers rose among the distinguished men in the meeting. For weeks they had argued and debated, deliberated and contested, discussed and questioned a formal statement of principles as an expression of the American mind.

"Together, as free men from each of the separate colonies, as voices of our citizenry, our families, our neighbors, we have set forth a list of grievances against the laws of a government which no longer represents our rights as human beings. We shall from here forward live under the laws of nature and the self-evident truths endowed by our Creator. We shall endure tyranny no longer and live by certain unalienable rights. Among these are life, liberty, and the pursuit of happiness."

The likes of John Adams, John Hancock, and Benjamin Franklin, along with the other fifty two colonial statesmen, had put their differences aside and showed their support for the document they were about to sign, one of the 'greatest statements of human liberty ever written.'

"In the name of the good people of the colonies, as unified peoples under divine Providence, we shall declare our independence and our right to be absolved of all allegiance to the British Crown.

"I ask you, gentlemen and statesmen," Thomas Jefferson concluded. "Shall we at this moment in history side with one another, pledge our lives, our fortunes, and our honor, in declaring our faithfulness to a new land governed by the people and for the people?"

From the preamble of author's book,
    Treasonous Behavior—In the Beginning

Find Your Purpose

We usually forget how fortunate we are living in America. In comparison to most of the world we are surrounded by wealth and opportunities and secured rights and privileges. We tend to take for granted our relatively easy and comfortable lives. We don't think much about the problems outside our windows, our towns, or our limited world view. But of course there are concerns out there.

I often talk about the three pillars of strength that made this country so wonderful. They are what built this land, what allows us to enjoy the hard work of our predecessors, what we are indeed privileged to enjoy without thinking about it. These major principals are our historic legacies

.

Free Will

They include the concept of free-will, which allows us to do anything we want to do. Here, the only limits placed upon ourselves are those limits we accept and bow to. Opportunity abounds in our country and we are mostly confined by our personal inner doubt, our lack of concerted effort, or our lack of knowledge.

Self-Determination

The second tenet of American greatness is self-determination. Every one of us has the possibility of being anyone we desire to be. We have the autonomy to become who we want to be, rich or poor, good or bad, educated or not. We have the freedom of determining our own destiny, our future, and our life goals. But of course, none of this comes without a cost. And that leads us to the third and most difficult concept of our on-going magnificence.

Rugged Individualism

Rugged individualism is the test of determination, the truth of persistence, the notion that anything is possible if you are diligent. It's a survivor's creed which instilled the building of great cities and unimaginable inventions and impossible adventures and resolute leaders. It pushes people to never give up despite grave odds. It encourages people to go beyond their human capabilities. It motivates people to risk their all for future and long-lasting benefits. It's the hard, dirty, scary work that many don't want to attempt, while those courageous individuals who do take the challenge reap the rewards.

These three ideas of sacrifice and perseverance and unending optimism are the core concepts of success. As Americans we have been given a fantastic gift of possibilities passed down through the generations. It is our individual responsibility to reach out, to accept the challenges, to decide to do something worthwhile. This workbook identifies the solid soft skills that are required to achieve such heights. Don't give up on yourselves. Learn and work to become who you want to be and to do what you want to do.

From author's book, *The Power of Soft Skills—*
50 Top Soft Skills for Success

Old Man Walking

Every morning while driving to work I would see this old man walking on the sidewalk coming my way. He appeared to be seventy-five, maybe eighty-years old. He had a difficult time making his daily routine while attempting to steady himself with a walking stick. He moved slowly but continued his walk, occasionally glancing up at where he was going.

The first couple of days I didn't pay very much attention to the guy. After all, I was in a rush to pick up my coffee at the Starbucks around the corner and get into work on time. There were other people on foot along both sides of the two-lane road as well. Some casually moseyed about without a care in the world, enjoying the sun's rays on their faces or preparing in their minds a list of things to do for the day. They looked retired, having nothing better to do with their mornings.

Others marched down the street flailing their arms and legs in a weird sort of rapid swinging exercise. A few morning joggers, immersed in their own world filled with music penetrating their ears, intent on their own cardiovascular workout, sprinted pass the pedestrians as if they were moving in slow motion.

The late spring air was still cool enough to warrant wearing a light jacket. I commuted the few miles into town. In my rear view mirror I could still see a thick layer of snow covering the mountain peaks behind me like a mottled white cotton blanket. In the Arizona high deserts snow could stick to the rugged pine-thick mountains well into late May even with the valley temperatures reaching into the eighties.

About the fifth day I noticed the old gentleman shuffling along the sidewalk carrying one of those small shiny oxygen tank canisters in one hand while deftly maneuvering his way with his wooden cane. A long clear air hose with a plastic mouthpiece was strapped over his mouth and nose, making it easier for him to breathe. The man obviously had some major health issues. Old age, the so called Golden Years, can be cruel.

In his condition he probably shouldn't be out doing such a strenuous task, I thought to myself.

For no apparent reason I decided to wave to the guy. A simple friendly gesture to some old geezer I didn't know. A little sign of human acknowledgement and perhaps even compassion on my part to a fellow citizen. It was completely uncharacteristic of me. Hey, I'm a busy guy. I have an important job, a big house, lots of friends, and I make a damn good income too. But while watching the man make his way, step by excruciatingly slow step, something inside me told me to wave.

What could it hurt? I thought. What's the worst that could happen? He wouldn't see me, or if he did see me with those old eyes of his maybe he would simply snub me and not even acknowledge my gracious signal. Old people do that sometimes.

Oh my god! How hurtful, how upsetting and insensitive, how typical that would be in such a modern cynical society where people stick to themselves and generally don't like to get involved with others outside their circle of influence. I'd probably do the exact same thing if I were in his shoes. There are peculiar strangers everywhere you turn. Besides, who really cares? Why do *I* have to step up and spread the joy? I have enough damn joy in my life, thank you very much.

So, against my better judgment as I was driving I stuck my hand up toward the windshield and waved at the elderly fart, as if he was a buddy of mine who I haven't seen since the last war. I think I actually cracked a small smile in the process.

It didn't even hurt.

To my surprise the grandfatherly man, sucking in his oxygen through the clumsy contraption, looked up at me and saw my less than enthusiastic hand motion. He stopped for a second to rest at the street corner and leaned against a metal stop sign post.

You won't believe what he did next.

No, he didn't blow me off, or flip me a crooked middle finger in an attempt to teach this young whippersnapper a thing or two about leaving people alone and minding my own damn Ps and Qs. He didn't shake his white curly head, partly covered by a tattered old cap, as if I was a nuisance, or worse yet, a real idiot.

Instead, this old gentleman did something that was totally unexpected.

He waved back at me.

A genuine smile unintentionally filled my otherwise typically smug face. I was sort of shocked, but in an amusing way. For a brief moment I wasn't concerned with standing in a long line to order my grande coffee. I wasn't thinking about the problems waiting for me at the office, the tons of e-mails which had to be answered, the files that had to be reviewed.

I just thought that, hey, he's a nice guy.

For some reason everything just seemed to go right that day. Work was fine and relatively uneventful, and far less dramatic than I had anticipated. Despite the late traffic the ride home was pleasant and I caught myself singing along with the radio. It was an absolute delight to enter my house to kiss my terrific wife and play with my two boys who were anxiously waiting for dinner.

Funny how some days turn out right for no particular reason.

Over the next several days I looked forward to seeing the old man walking along the same stretch of sidewalk. He must have lived in one of the houses nearby since it was apparent there was no way he could walk very far.

Around seven o'clock in the morning, every day, give or take a minute, I would see him and he would notice me in my shiny new blue car. We both waved at one another like good friends do, like we'd known each other for years.

I swear, some mornings it seemed he was waiting on the corner for me to slowly approach and say hello with a cheerful wave. It was kind of like he was looking forward to our daily non-verbal exchange. And frankly, it wasn't a bad part of my trip either.

Since I really didn't know him, and of course had no idea what his name was, I began to privately call him 'George,' which I've always thought was a good, solid, strong name for such a gentleman.

"Hey George," I'd shout out as I waved toward him from inside my vehicle.

From a distance 'George' sort of reminded me of my dad who had long since passed away, except 'George' was a bit thinner and more bent over than my father. But nevertheless he did resemble my dad. I guess lots of old people tend to look alike. I wanted to stop my car and get out and talk to this man, learn more about him, find out how he was doing.

But of course I couldn't do that. It would be too odd, too uncomfortable.

I'd have to say that this quiet encounter went on for about a month or so. "Hello George," I would yell out and touch my hand to the inside of my windshield. He always waved back at me with a slow, old man motion, and smiled the best he could. I came to enjoy seeing him and really thought he liked the traveling camaraderie too, if only for a brief second, five days a week.

Each passing day as the weather warmed up it seemed 'George' was moving a bit slower, struggling a little more to finish the short trip around his block. He seemed to be a nice old man doing his thing the best he could, unpretentious in his soft white sneakers and baggy pants. At least he was outdoors, getting some sun and a bit of fresh air, I reasoned. At least he wasn't stuck in front of a television set nodding off through sheer desperate boredom.

At least 'George' was out there, still in the game.

Then one day I didn't see him on his usual route.

The next day he wasn't there either.

Or the next.

After that I never saw the old man again, my waving buddy. I didn't know what had happened to my friend 'George,' but I could guess.

Three days later I was sitting at my desk reading the local newspaper. There was a grainy picture of 'George' on page six. It was a photograph of a much younger man, but I still recognized him. The obituary was quite long and apparently had been written by someone who loved the man dearly and knew him well.

'George's real name was Herman S. Polinsky and he was born in 1922, which made him eighty-eight years old. As a young man he had attended Harvard University in Cambridge, Massachusetts where he earned his engineering degree. He had worked for various private government contractors and had even invented several innovative fuel system relays used in the later NASA space flights.

'George' Herman had served in the U.S. Army as a captain during World War II, mostly in the European Theatre. He was twice wounded by enemy fire in the invasion of Normandy, for which he was decorated with two Purple Heart medals. He was a full bird colonel in the

Korean Conflict and received several commendations and medals for his meritorious service to his beloved country.

After having retired in Arizona the man also had published three books on the natural wildlife of the Southwest. He was a lifelong member of the Audubon Society, the Rotary Club, the Elks Lodge, and other service clubs. Prior to his death he had volunteered his time at the local city library and Senior Center.

I stopped reading and looked out my office window. There were phones ringing in the background, people walking back and forth through the office building, doors opening and closing. I just stared blankly into the blue desert sky.

I felt small.

According to the farewell biography 'George' was preceded in death by his wife of fifty-three years, Elsie. His five brothers and two sisters had also gone before him. He was survived by his four sons, eleven grandchildren, and seventeen great-grandchildren.

'George' would be missed by many.

I should wave at more people.

Prologue from Treasonous Behavior

It's a naturally, and frequently, occurring phenomenon which under ideal conditions can kill nearly every human being on the planet. It's called an Electromagnetic Pulse, commonly referred to as an EMP.

An Electromagnetic Pulse occurs by natural forces emitted from our solar source, some ninety-three million miles from earth. These solar flares are produced by an abrupt release of magnetic fields stored within the gaseous core of the sun. The huge amounts of energy released can reach the equivalent of 160,000,000 megatons of TNT. The recurrent fiery explosions eject invisible clouds of charged electrons and ions upwards to heights of nearly 500,000 kilometers. Flare-up temperatures can reach highs of 100,000,000 degrees Kelvin.

Corona mass eruptions from the outermost atmospheres of the sun trigger geometric storms sending pulsating waves of destruction throughout our solar system. X1 class events, the most severe storms emitted from the sun peaking in eleven year solar cycles, quickly distort the ionosphere. The imperceptible effect of the EMP reaches the earth with the speed of light producing radiation across the entire electromagnetic spectrum.

It is one of the most devastatingly destructive attacks on a planet and its inhabitants imaginable. At over 186,000 miles per second an EMP hits its targets without warning. On earth's surface it strangely causes no perceptible colossal explosion. It creates no menacing fireballs, no torrential wind storms, no massive flooding, no destructive earthquakes. It destroys no houses, no buildings, no infrastructure. It swiftly and silently sweeps through cities and villages, fields and farms, leaving no discernable damage. It leaves no lasting effect on earth's plant life, its forests, or sea life. It directly injures no animals, nor openly kills a single human being. It is neither seen, heard, nor felt by its unfortunate victims. Yet it is still the most deadly force ever envisioned.

Electronic waves a million times more powerful than any radio signal on the planet destroys all electronic devices in its path. All power grids turn off as if a simple switch were suddenly flipped. Like a silent weapon the EMP carries with it damaging voltage surges burning out semi-conductor chips in any electrical equipment within its line of sight. Every one of the more than 300,000,000 personal computers and laptops in America will shut down within a fraction of second.

All forms of telecommunication ends. Three hundred thirty million cell phones power down in the blink of an eye. Hard wired land phones fail, radios go silent, televisions go dark. Untold numbers, perhaps billions of memory microchips, logic circuitry, SIM cards, and integrated circuits cease to function as the unseen pulse of death burns up the magical powers of silicon innovation. Every technologically advanced digitized piece of equipment and energized system developed over the last decades instantly become useless hunks of metal and plastic.

All means of land transportation screech to a sudden halt without warning. Millions of automobiles and pickups slow to a stop. Commercial haulers charge forward with their weighted momentum, crashing into stationary structures. Police cruisers, city buses, fire engines, and motorcycles stop dead in the streets.

Tens of thousands of accidents occur at the same moment. City intersections become massive pile ups as thousands of traffic lights go down and engines fail to respond. Law enforcement and military vehicles as well, become disabled, failing to respond to cries of help and increasing chaos. Millions of motorists become confused, angered, disoriented, stranded at their work places or from their homes.

Freight trains pulling miles of loaded containers coast to a long but quiet stop. Passenger trains traveling cross country end up forsaken in the open scrub western deserts or the flat central plains of America. Packed commuter trains speeding along the metro corridor between Washington, DC and New York City roll to an end of their journey, still far from their destinations. Subway trains deep beneath the asphalt of Chicago and Boston and New York leave their hundreds of thousands of travelers isolated in the pitch black maze of tunnels.

Ships hit by the pulse drift aimlessly without power. Monstrous oil tankers run aground in the Gulf of Mexico. Cargo ships entering ports on both the east and west coasts float helplessly in the ocean currents. Cruise ships out of Miami flounder without purposeful direction. Naval aircraft carriers, cruisers, and battleships lie dormant in the San Diego and Newport News shipyards, unable to protect our shores. Pleasure boats and decked-out yachts float adrift in open waters.

Within seconds every aircraft in flight goes quiet and falls to earth. More than five thousand planes, including commercial airliners, private craft, air cargo carriers, helicopters, and military jets, are in the air at any given time over the skies of the United States. All are instantly doomed as the powerful pulse ruptures their vulnerable systems. Redundant backup systems fail just as easily.

At an attitude of 35,000 feet, a cross country jetliner instantly loses power to its engines. Seasoned pilots frantically attempt to restart the turbines, but with no working controls their efforts prove useless. Hundreds of passengers strapped in their seats scream in horror when the lights go out and their plane begins to drop like a stone. Travelers and flight crew have a mere forty-six seconds to pray before they crash into the earth. Hundreds of thousands of other air passengers meet the same fate as planes hopelessly drop from the sky simultaneously.

Elevators in large apartment houses, office buildings, and government centers stop mid-floor. Some free fall straight to crushing death. With no lights, no working phones, and no manner of escape, the poor souls remain in their stainless steel coffins. Heart pacemakers shut down, killing seniors blindly. Hospital ventilators stop ventilating patients. Critical monitors quit monitoring. Life saving devices cease saving.

Every financial institution in the land is affected. Banks turn dark and completely unprotected. Alarm systems become worthless deterrents. All credit cards and debit cards and wire transfers are ended in mid-transaction. The New York Stock Exchange streams into mayhem as the giant money boards dim. Every company stock and every corporate or government bond simply vanishes into thin air. All bank account amounts disappear into cyberspace, as if they never existed. Savings and checking and pension plans are instantaneously wiped out, as if they never registered. Every dollar of government funding ceases to exist. No financial record in the path of the EMP survives.

All retail stores in the country lock down without operating computers. Throughout the nation, grocery stores hurry customers out of their businesses as the registers bind up, the frozen foods begin to melt, and the perishable products begin to sour and decay. Food soon becomes a major concern.

In all homes and businesses, apartments and civic buildings, the electricity shuts off as the power grids burn out. Even daylight turns dark in residences and workplaces. Water pipes run dry, natural gas for heating quits delivery, refrigerators turn warm as houses turn cold in the lasting winter cold.

Every single factor of modern living comes to an end in an instant. A total shutdown of the computerized age takes hold. Digital progress disintegrates. Within seconds of a solar electromagnetic pulse an entire advanced civilization is thrown back some two hundred years to when kerosene lit houses and steam drove machines. A thriving, rich country, once the envy of the world, becomes paralyzed and unprotected, people dying from the effects of an unseen force, and the rest running scared to death in anticipation of what might be coming next.

Most people are ill-prepared for such a catastrophic disaster. Only days after the EMP strikes people run out of drinking water and turn to their toilets. Meager pantry food supplies are exhausted in two weeks' time. Food, once plentiful, becomes a precious commodity. Medications are used up as patients gasp for air or fall to chest pains. Families are separated, most likely never to be reunited. News of the event remains nonexistent for the lack of power. Cries for help go unanswered and mayhem sets in and is common.

People panic and live in fear. Alarm and chaos rule the day. People die from dehydration, then from starvation. Soon others fail from untreated ailments. First the elderly and the sick, then young children. The devastation and lack of electricity continues for at least six months, perhaps much longer. Should the systems which inhabitants and businesses and governments once so casually relied on stay shut down for a full year, almost ninety percent of the American population will perish from starvation, disease, or societal chaos, and its ensuing collapse.

But the normal phenomenon of solar flares is not the worst catastrophe inflicted upon an unprepared nation.

Solar disturbances are but one cause of an EMP, a regular occurrence completely beyond control of mankind. Scientists, astronomers, and astrophysicists monitor and study the sun's surface, constantly fearful of a massive flare up, a giant sunspot which can shoot out six times the diameter of the earth. World leaders aware of the catastrophic potential, pray a solar induced electromagnetic pulse will never come to pass on their watch. Common citizens following their mundane and trivial days ignore the possibility entirely.

Equally devastating, though by far vastly more abhorrent than any other devious act of man conceived in history, is when an EMP is intentionally triggered. A first possible scenario is an EMP being created by sophisticated and well-funded enemies of a state intent on paralyzing its foe.

In the midst of the Dark Ages the widespread outbreak of the insidious black plague killed a mere fraction of those who could be wiped out by a strategically initiated EMP. Over a thousand centuries of man butchering his own kind pale in the shadow of an EMP aftermath. Millions were slaughtered during the Great Crusades. Millions more were massacred by the dictators of oppressed countries. Millions again were selectively eradicated by mad men in power, or starved to death by obsessed rulers intent on self-idolization, or enslaved and annihilated by fanatical godless men. Such historic carnage in total would barely reach the potential death toll of a single electromagnetic pulse perfectly executed.

An EMP event over the central plains of the United States would cause a staggering death toll of the American population. Upwards of 300,000,000 people on the continent would die from the long term aftermath effects of an intentional EMP explosion. There would be no bloodshed, no shots fired, no traditional killing, no death by standard warfare.

Instead, the millions of citizens—men, women, and children—would perish from ultimate starvation, pervasive diseases, and eventual societal disintegration. In the hands of a radical group determined to annihilate the United

States, an electromagnetic pulse would be the perfect weapon.

Russia's military has largely been dismantled since the breaking up of the Soviet Union. However, it still has the capability to slip a stealth nuclear submarine within a few miles of the American coasts and deploy a missile over the American continent. Russia would have no qualms in attempting to wipe out the western superpower in its striving to gain super status once again.

A top secret Russian strategic submarine known as the SSBM, slips beneath the calm waters of the Gulf of Mexico fifty miles off the shores of New Orleans. It carries a one megaton nuclear warhead on the tip of a medium range ballistic missile. This specially designed weapon is an enhanced super EMP, or E-bomb.

The missile is aimed near the center of the continental United States, over the Nebraska-Kansas border, approximately one thousand miles in distance from the Gulf. Once deployed, it takes the missile only six and a half minutes to meet its target, too quick for U.S. domestic defenses to react. The nuclear device explodes two-hundred miles above its ideal coordinates. The High Altitude EMP will have an effective range of over fifteen hundred miles rippling across the nation. It spreads into the southern portions of Canada and the northern sections of Mexico. The vast American shorelines of the Pacific and Atlantic Oceans and hundreds of miles of sea beyond will be affected as well. Most of the Gulf of Mexico will also be covered by the pulse. Results of the intentional attack will be similar to those caused by a solar flare EMP, only more sinister.

Except, it would open America to even more devastation. It would clear the path for Russia's other mortal enemy, China, to stand tall in the number one spot of worldwide domination.

Of course China, the Red Dragon, with its huge, unmatched military force, could initiate its own assault against America. Its advanced EMP bombs are aimed at the eastern seaboard of the United States—the political, financial, and defense centers of the country. Long-range intercontinental missiles or nuclear liftoffs from nearby secluded submarines could inevitably give Communist China the edge they have long desired. Such an injured nation could easily succumb to an invading naval force and savage takeover.

In the end, China would lose its prominent economic trader, its favored trading status, its monetized security on trillions owed it by the U.S. But China would gain much, much more.

Another rogue, dogmatic nation, North Korea, has secured the technology from Russia capable of launching ICBMs carrying 300 kiloton nuclear bombs. They are able to fire a preemptive long-range nuclear missile orbiting over the South Pole, and detonating it over specific regions of the North American continent.

Iran is another nation with an intense hatred toward the West, and in particular against Americans. It and any number of mobile terrorist groups are ever preparing to pull the trigger to annihilate the White Devil once and for all in an attempt to fulfill their prophetic destiny.

The world is full of American enemies ready to eradicate the Great Satan. Most of them foreign, many of them domestic. But, there are even more malicious forces determined to stamp out the American way, if that is even feasible. As enemies within, they will eventually reveal their heinous and treasonous behavior to the astonishment of the American people and those who thought it could never happen.

Which leads to the second possibility of an EMP being deliberately activated.

It is something beyond comprehension to the average citizen. It shows the true evil nature of man in the pursuit of power and riches. With the backing of a small group of insiders, a leader of a nation resolute to use weapons of unspeakable destruction against his own people for his own designing agenda, could accomplish it. Such vile actions can only be halted if the citizens of a nation remain vigilant against the inherent wickedness of man and decide to take control of their own fate.

There is only one question to ponder.

Will the people stand up to such terror?

From author's *Treasonous Behavior—In the Beginning*

"If I Can Read..."

"Why are you here?" he abruptly asked the unexpected question.

All eyes looked at him with surprised expressions. Then the students squirmed in their seats. Some looked down at their notebooks. Others fiddled with their sharpened pencils. A few turned to their closest classmates. A couple brave ones stared at the Teacher without a clue as to what he was asking.

The classroom was filled with twenty-two new students. All the available seats were taken as the entire group remained quiet. The Teacher looked at each of his students one by one, focusing on the confused and perhaps frightened faces for excruciating long seconds as he moved around the room and the crowded tables set in a large U-shape configuration facing the front of the room.

No doubt every student immediately thought about what they had gotten themselves into. This Teacher was mean, they collectively thought. School was supposed to be fun, enjoyable, rewarding. This is not what they expected. A few students even considered getting up and leaving the room, but it would be an embarrassing move.

The Teacher asked again, this time in a friendlier, almost fatherly tone, "Why are you here?" He let the question simmer for a minute. He knew how this worked. He'd done it many times before. Let them think for a moment, and then the answers would come.

A middle-aged Korean lady shyly raised her hand and responded, "I want learn English." Most of the students nodded their agreement in unison, encouraging others to speak up as well.

"I need English," a broad-shouldered man in his forties added.

"I must English for a job," a young Vietnamese boy said with a sense of despair.

The tension in the brightly lit room seemed to ease a bit. "English is necessary here in America," a well-spoken student offered his opinion. More heads nodded yes. By now every person in the room was watching the Teacher as he slowly walked back and forth knowing precisely what he was going to say next.

"I know all that," the Teacher said.

His voice was calm but somewhat disappointed. "This is an English class. I understand that you want to learn English, that English is important to you," he said. "But I still want to know why you are really here."

He let the repeated question rest. His students would get it. They would figure out what he was really asking. They always did, because deep inside every one of them held their real reasons.

Seconds later things began to click. "I want to be a citizen," one student said, "but I have a hard time reading."

The Teacher looked at him with a smile. The first smile of the day. "Good one," he said as he pointed approvingly toward the young lady.

"My children in school and I need to talk to teacher," another one said in broken but passable English. The mother sat back in her seat, happy that she had voiced her explanation the best she could.

The Teacher acknowledged the mother's needs, "I know exactly what you mean. That's important to you, right?"

She may not have understood every word he said, but she understood enough to give a big smile and a hardy positive headshake.

"I want to drive," an older woman shouted out. "I want to go shopping by myself! I no like waiting for a friend or my husband to drive me. He no like shopping." The whole class broke out in laughter. It was a very common reason to learn and study English.

"Oh yes!" the Teacher shouted. He'd heard this many times in his classrooms. "What are some other reasons you want to learn English?" he asked the group, roaming amongst the students.

"College," someone said. "I need better English to go to college. In my home country I was a veterinarian, but here I need more school."

The Teacher grinned and simply nodded his approval. "It's not very easy, is it? Trying to pick up where you left off. You have an education and it means little in America. School is important. Improving your English skills is important. Don't ever stop learning. Don't ever forget what you really want."

More hands were raised.

The students, who less than ten minutes earlier were ready to jump ship, now were beginning to like this Teacher. Nobody had ever before asked these people what they really wanted out of life. At home growing up they were told what to do. In school they were handed routine assignments and told to simply complete them without asking questions. In their jobs—for those who had jobs—their particular wants and needs and desires were of no importance. Their sole purpose was to just work, do what their boss told them, and collect their meager paychecks.

But something was different about this class, this Teacher. He wanted to know what they wanted, what they needed. He wanted to know why. It was a given that English would be thoroughly taught in his classroom, but he wanted to understand the motivation of each of his new students. That was the key to them learning and growing. He absolutely believed it.

Coming to class three days a week for three-hour classes wasn't easy, or convenient. These were adult foreign students, typically ranging in ages from twenty to upwards of seventy or even seventy-five. They had busy lives. They had families to care for. They had work to deal with. They had expenses outpacing their incomes. Near the end of the month some of them couldn't come to class because they didn't have the bus fare or couldn't put gas in their car. They had child care issues and broken down cars and education concerns. They had cultural differences and obvious language problems. And then there was discrimination, in-your-face bigotry and unspoken prejudices. These were people, good people, who constantly lived on the edge.

But the Teacher knew his students' greatest obstacles. He had seen them out in the open and hidden behind humble and stoic faces. He had worked with them enough over the years to see what really bothered them. It was something that few people ever recognized and fewer took into account. His students needed to learn to believe in themselves. They needed to develop a sense of self-reliance and self-confidence and having the ability to be in control of their lives. They needed to believe in their future.

That was the Teacher's job.

To help them believe.

That's what he did.

"I want a job," one student eagerly said as if he had someone finally on his side.

"I want a better job," added his neighbor.

"I want to make lots of money," a thin man from South America said.

The entire class clapped in agreement.

The Teacher quickly jumped on the last statement. Keep them talking, he thought. Let them open up. "Why do you want more money?" he asked the man with a thick accent.

"Because I want a girlfriend," he laughed. "And they cost a lot of money!"

Everyone, including the Teacher, cracked up. He had discovered the clown in the class. There was always at least one, and that was good. Humor was a welcomed relief in the classroom.

"That's very true," the Teacher said. "Women can be very expensive."

There was another uproar in the class. The ice had been broken and a true connection was in progress.

"What else?" the Teacher inquired of the noticeably at-ease students. Hands were waging high in the air. Enthusiasm was necessary in a learning environment too.

"I want help my children with homework," a middle-aged mother from Sonora, Mexico said.

"I want save money to visit my home," a man from Ecuador added.

A young girl who had only weeks arrived in America said proudly, "I want to be a nurse."

"I want to send money to my mother," another student said.

"I want have a better car," a tall skinny kid about twenty years old said.

"I want to retire early," the class clown chuckled. He looked around the room waiting for his audience to react.

"You need to have a job first," the Teacher answered.

The man just grinned his big sociable smile, as if to say, 'I know.'

This was fun.

The Teacher went to the front whiteboard and picked up a blue marker. "Let's make a list of some of the reasons you are really here in class."

And he wrote on top of the board and read it out loud.

WHY I WANT TO LEARN ENGLISH

One by one he handed a colored marker to each student and asked them to approach the board and write down their reasons. Some, of course, were reluctant or ashamed of their writing skills, or simply too scared to go in front of the class of strangers. The ones who willingly went to the board began writing their wants and dreams. Many of the words were misspelled or missing or a mixture of English and their native language, but they got their ideas across.

When they were done there was a list of about twenty reasons they wanted to improve their English. They were familiar to the Teacher because he had seen them all before. For the most part all people wanted the same things in life and this group of students was no different. The Teacher noticed one item was missing, so on the board he added it to the end of the list:

SELF-CONFIDENCE

That word triggered another rising of the hands.

"I want to know I can do something," one student said.

"I want feel good inside," an older student mumbled.

"I want be free," another said.

"Exactly," the Teacher said. "These are things you want, but you must first learn English. First things first. You will learn and you will get better. It may take some time but you will get there. I am here to help you, and together we will grow and you will get a job or a better job. You will make more money and be able to send money home to your family. You will be able to talk with your children's teachers and help them with their homework. You will have a better car or a nicer home. You will be able to go to college, to be a nurse or veterinarian or teacher or whatever you want to be. You will have a better life."

The Teacher looked at the class clown and said jokingly, "You may even be able to afford a girlfriend someday."

Everyone laughed again.

"And yes," the Teacher paused to get his students' attention, because this was serious. "You will feel good about yourself. You will control your life. You will have respect and you will be confident."

The class sat still.

No one moved.

No one spoke.

They just looked at the long list of possibilities in front of them. They looked at their Teacher as if they truly believed there were changes about to happen.

And there were.

"There is one thing I want to remind each and every one of you," the Teacher said.

He turned to the board and wrote a short sentence. Without saying a word a few students opened their notebooks or borrowed a piece of paper. Then the rest of the class did the same. They all picked up their freshly sharpened pencils and copied the saying from the board, as if it held the answers to all their questions.

The Teacher knew that today they may not all believe what it said. But in a short time more students would believe, and ideally by the end of the semester, all twenty-two new students would know what they had written to be a fact.

The Teacher read the sentence slowly to his new and promising students:

"IF I CAN READ, I CAN DO ANYTHING!"

The Partners

The business partners exited their office building through the back door. "We need a short break from all of this," the older gentleman said as he walked toward his shiny new car at the far end of the long parking lot. "I already have a friggin' headache."

"Don't complain. This is what we wanted. Just a half hour away from the desk, enough to clear our heads and catch our breath," the other man agreed with his friend as he followed him with great anticipation. He closed and locked the rear courtyard security gates to prevent anybody from surprising their secretary through the back entrance.

It was another busy day for the ambitious middle-aged entrepreneurs. A day to change all days. Their ingenious and somewhat outrageous business concepts had caught on fire. They were innovative and genuine. Controversial was probably the best word to describe them, yet it was right there in the Code. Radical, some people called it.

It was clear as day that what they were doing was allowed by those who had established the rules, but it was never offered. It was supposedly written for the protection of the public, but conveniently never disclosed. Most likely, both men believed, because of the general pervasiveness of ignorance and avarice of the majority of members of the so-called club. A club to which the boys did not want to belong, didn't even want to be associated with.

The average consumer hated the club, had little respect for its members, looked upon them as a necessary evil, and only hired them as a last resort. The guys hated the club even more because they knew how it worked. They knew of the back room dealings and the ultimate agenda of most every licensed member. They knew of the rampant incompetence and the underlying greed that had taken over what was once a respectable vocation. It had evolved into a sham promoted by the governing agencies. It was a damned shame what it had gradually turned into. The whole industry was indeed inherently evil.

The real reason, though, that such a plan was never implemented was because no one in the business had the balls to promote it. After all, it most certainly took courage to buck the system and turn the rules against the very members for whom they were created to protect. The men were in for the fight of their lives against local, state, and national policies. They thought they were ready, but if the truth were to be told they might have never attempted to attack the system if they could have envisioned the uphill battle they would encounter.

It was an epic of David and Goliath proportions. The competition would soon learn of the pioneers' commitment and passion for their new way of running a real estate firm. For them failure was not an option. Everyone who knew them would agree the partners had balls. Big balls.

Why hadn't anyone else ever offered such a radical but so logical a solution to the needs and desires of so many clients? It was shocking but so obvious. Millions of clients, if the numbers identified by the national association could be believed, would be affected. Who knew there would be such an overwhelming, pent-up demand? Well, the partners knew. They saw the future. Or at least they had hoped there would be such a demand for their services when they had stepped way out and invented and promoted their plan. So far it seemed everyone liked what the men were doing.

Well, not everyone.

The phones were ringing off the hook. It was apparent more phone lines were needed. They needed more help out front also. Two more assistants would do. Angela, the frantic receptionist, was doing the best she could but it was impossible for her to handle the barrage of incoming calls all by herself. Other agents had to be recruited too, but the question was who out there in the pathetic field of potential prospects could handle the pressure and not cave in to the inevitable scorn of the rest of the industry. Experienced agents with thick skin and a driving urge to do something exciting and different were needed. The problem was, there were very few, if any, out there who could stand the heat and maintain their resolve to persevere when the shit hit the fan.

And it most definitely would hit.

Appointments were scheduled for every hour of the day, twelve hours each and every day. Even on Sunday. Sometimes they were doubled up because of the incredible response. The small front lobby was always crammed with clients and customers wanting to get their precious hour in front of either partner. It wasn't unusual to see a line of people streaming out the main entrance doors into the front parking lot impatiently waiting their turn.

Even when the two men arrived at work as early as six o'clock in the morning to catch up on stacks of paperwork and new files, there were some early risers knocking on the front door to find out more about the unbelievable program the independent agents had devised.

The owners would sneak in through the rear and not turn on the receptionist area or hallway lights so they could at least settle in and suck down a quick cup of coffee in peace before the overbearing influx of home sellers and buyers entered the office. What had they done? The answer was—exactly what they had intended to do. Their plan was most definitely working. Maybe too well.

Later in the day, around lunch time, the blond man pointed and clicked the remote to open his driver's side door.

....TICK...

They were just going for a quick sandwich away from the crowded office. The car was cleaned and polished under the cool shade of Japanese maples lining the back lot. He took a moment to admire the large magnetic sign attached to the side door panel advertising their bold idea in an otherwise conventional business. "Expect To Sell Discount Real Estate." He smiled at the eye-catching lettering and registered logo. "Now that's sharp," he said out loud as he neared the vehicle.

Unknown to the partners a homemade bomb had been strapped to the bottom of the car's gas tank, wired to explode once the ignition was activated. The mystery bomber had parked his truck next to the partner's car in mid-morning, stealthily placed the explosive in the most vulnerable position, and beneath the vehicle hurriedly wired the denotation device. It took him less than two minutes to plant the deadly package. He was noticed by no one.

"Oh, hell!" the forty-five year old man said, realizing he had forgotten the file. He and his partner were going to review their new programs and charts over lunch. They had more plans that would continue to change their industry. Changes their clients hungered for. Things that were never done before.

It was about time, the younger man thought to himself. "We will make this work," he said, then turned to his partner. "You dumb shit," he jokingly yelled at his buddy as he returned to unlock the gate.

"I'll just be a minute," he told his friend as the gate was swung open.

After retrieving the folder he casually remarked, "Sorry about that." The gate was quickly re-locked.

...TICK...TICK...

Two full sticks of dynamite were tightly wrapped together around the detonator with duct tape. It was enough explosives to wipe out everything within a hundred-foot radius. The red ignition wire was spliced into the bomb waiting for a simple turn of the key to send a small spark through the coil and into the device. It was a compact but deadly charge and most assuredly would get the job done. That's what the bomber was being paid for.

"You'd forget your head if it wasn't attached," his buddy ribbed him.

"Right now I probably would," the man nodded.

The two men walked to within fifty feet of the car. They were both tired but exhilarated with their work. Being different is what they were all about.

The older man clicked his remote again.

...TICK...TICK...TICK...

Click-click. The remote activated and released the door locks. An electrical discharge carried through the thin wire down to the detonator into the dual nitroglycerin sticks. The car bomb took less than a second to erupt but it was premature since the dumb shit who rigged it to the undercarriage had mistakenly wired it to the door release solenoid instead of the ignition. Sometimes mistakes cost lives. This one saved them.

It was a nice sunny spring day, the high Arizona noon sun warmed the air. A refreshing cool breeze floated down the valley off the rugged mountains from the south which separated the United States from Mexico. Remnants of winter snow clung to the highest rugged peaks. Birds were chirping in the low-hanging trees near the car. It was quiet and peaceful, unlike the mad rush in back in the office.

KABOOM!

Without warning, the car exploded. The tremendous blast blew the men hard to the concrete pavement as if they were toppled over by a fierce tornado. A solid wave of intense heat radiated from the explosion's core and hit the partners dead on. The molten air singed their eyebrows and the hair on their arms only partly protected by their short-shelve shirts. A giant ball of red and yellow flames soared above their head. The acrid smell of burning fuel and oil and leather immediately assaulted the downed men. An ugly thick rising plume of black-gray smoke choked the noon sky. The two dazed agents stayed low on the hot ground mere steps from the raging firebomb.

Burning chunks of Buick fell around the intended victims. Millions of pieces of searing pellet glass rained on them and the surrounding area. Melting shreds of tires and seats and rubber hoses cascaded on the two as they scurried away from the inferno. Jagged, twisted metal parts rocketed ten stories into the sky and mortared their way back to the earth. The vehicle had been ripped into a murderous hulk of flaming death.

Within seconds it had bounced ten feet off the pavement, rolled over, and flipped onto its roof, the underbelly burning and crackling from the tremendous explosion. The force of the immense blast scorched the parking lot and adjacent road in a perfect circle from its center. The trees closest to the car lit up like torches as the gas-fed flames lapped up the branches.

The stack of files in the partner's hand were blown from his grip and scattered in the wind. Some of the documents were sucked into the blaze and immediately destroyed by the hungry fire. Dozens of loose secrets littered the site.

The competition was ruthless.

Ben and Taylor, slightly singed, but barely scratched, picked themselves up from the devastation. Astonished, they looked at the mangled heap and the burning debris around them, then at each other. Ben was just getting to like his new car. Someone was going to pay. The men brushed themselves off, the anger in their eyes hotter than the bomb's blast, and turned back toward their office.

Lunch had just been cancelled.

The competition had expressed their concerns. It wasn't totally unexpected, but now the stakes had been raised and the partners knew what they had to do next.

Apparently new ideas were dangerous.

It was time to make a phone call.

Missing Pieces

Students are quickly falling behind in skills sought after by employers in today's competitive workplace. This includes younger students, junior and high school students, and particularly incoming college students.

Soft skills, more commonly known as people skills, such as time management, teamwork, accountability, innovation, and yes, even punctuality, are not being taught to our young people in preparation for their future.

Schools are focused on the basic three Rs, reading, writing, and 'rithmatic, and frankly, are not doing a very good job at that. Educators seem to be more concerned with test scores and regulations and classroom management and pushing tech rather than polishing soft skills and life skills as well.

Home life, for better or worse, is centered on the two income family in order to afford the American dream. Parents are overwhelmed with expectations to live the good life surrounded by things to make them happy. Families are crushed with debt and worried about the future. Children are too often left on their own to function without proper guidance and instruction. Solid life lessons and skills are infrequently passed on.

Social media has seriously invaded younger generations' lives. They have been disengaged from real life. They are socially accepted or rejected according to the number of 'friends' and 'likes' they generate. Business leaders report that three major soft skills such as communication, critical thinking, and interpersonal skills are particularly lacking. Many of these missing pieces in our youth's lives can be traced back to social media platforms.

My concern is not only with the failure to teach our next generations the importance of making plans in the form of effective goal setting, but also in the lack of dedication in honing character traits, personal attributes, the soft skills. They include a long list of personal, social, and professional qualities. These skills, when properly taught, can propel students far beyond their education level and hands-on experience in the hard skills.

Soft skills, the talents which actually make businesses run well, are quickly becoming key factors to success in one's career, as I state in my book, *The Power of Soft Skills—50 Top Soft Skills for Success.*

But what about life skills?

Many students don't have a clue when it comes to the day-to-day skills necessary to survive on their own.

Are young people taught how to properly handle credit and debt as they enter the adult world? Are they shown how to make large purchases such as a house or car? Are they aware of the needs and cautions to be taken when securing insurance? Are they able to manage a budget based on income and needs? Do they understand the significance of taxes in their lives? Are they educated in the wealth building principles of investing for the long term? Are they given the opportunity to take qualified risks in life? To make mistakes and learn from them? Are they taught to save for later expenses, or more importantly, for retirement? Are they told that sometimes in life they will lose? Are they allowed to gain true self-confidence, a sense of self-reliance, a perception of self-worth?

I think not.

It is truly frustrating to see these skills, both soft and life skills, being largely neglected by our education system and family environment.

Our young people will pay dearly for the error.

From author's post on Linked-in

Happy 24,455th Birthday!

In a not so momentous time last week I suddenly realized and recognized an outside the box epiphany. Time indeed does move quickly, and at certain intervals in our lives we tend to stop and look back at our accomplishments, if any. In my goal setting workbooks and classes I emphasize that we all should "Do Something!" every day.

"What have I done in the past days and years that have been worthwhile?" I asked myself. At least a few good things of value, I hope.

At 18 years old a young person has already been on this earth for 6570 days! In those few early years not much gets accomplished, but the path to your future, even though unclear, can at least be anticipated. Here begins the first steps of who you will become, what you will achieve, where you will go.

At 25, a person with 9125 days behind you, perhaps a recent graduate, a job seeker, or young parent, has typically established your path in life. Your future has already begun, and unless you truly focus on what it is you want in life, you are on the winding track either to success or mediocrity or failure. Now is the time to commit.

At 30 years, or about 10,950 days, you are typically in the struggling mode. Family, finances, debt, career choices, relationships, responsibilities. A bucket of self-doubt too. Are your efforts worthy of your goals? Are you following the right path? Do you remember what's most important as you near the half-way point?

At 50, some 18,250 days into your journey, you should be comfortable with your choices, well on your way to promised rewards. What have you done to be proud of? Who have you helped? Where have you gone? How have you made a difference? What have you contributed? These are questions which may bother you. It's still not too late.

At 65, the supposed golden age, day 23,725, you have made it to this envious milestone. But is it what you had hoped for and dreamt about? Perhaps. I hope so. The calendar is quickly catching up. If needed, change is still possible. Go do something good. More good is needed out there.

"Do Something!" fun and helpful and memorable and worthwhile. Make your life, no matter how many days have passed, extraordinary.

A Good Man

John Joseph Silva was born on October 24, 1929, what would soon become one of the most ominous days in the history of the United States of America. Most old timers, those who are still around, remember it as Black Thursday, the day the stock market crashed and pushed the country into the doldrums of The Great Depression.

That day was Johnny's birthright.

Just months earlier a young married couple by the name of John and Marta Silva had survived the long, arduous trip by steamship from their small home village south of Lisbon, Portugal. They had traveled to the New World in search of steady work and the dream they had so often read about. At the time Marta was several months pregnant with their first child.

Upon arriving in their new country they had settled in a community of other Portuguese immigrant families within the city of Somerville, which bordered on the northern edge of Boston. On Laurel Street they rented a small, dingy third floor apartment amongst hundreds of other look-a-like frame built triple-decker houses with the dangerously steep stairways and deteriorating wooden back balconies. The city was teeming with foreign settlers and newcomers all looking for work and a better life.

Life in America. It was difficult, but promising. What was one of the happiest days in John's and Marta's lives, the birth of their son, had turned out to be the most devastating time for their adopted country.

John Silva had been a meat cutter in the old country and got a job in one of the local butcher shops. The market district lining both sides of Somerville Ave was filled with fruit and produce vendors, Portuguese, Italian, and Jewish bakeries, mom and pop general stores, a variety of meat markets, cobbler shops, small taverns, family restaurants, and every other type of inner city enterprise. Marta, though only eighteen at the time, was an accomplished seamstress and worked, until she had the baby, sewing cotton shirts and trousers at a huge textile factory not far from their flat.

John, a third generation butcher, was fortunate to have a skill in demand. While millions were losing their jobs, thousands of businesses were shutting down, banks were closing, factories and manufacturing plants were drastically cutting back, and untold numbers of family farms were being foreclosed upon. Unemployment had risen to an unprecedented twenty-five percent.

But people still had to eat. Beef was selling for between twenty and thirty cents a pound, for those who could afford it. Milk was fourteen cents a quart, bread was nine cents a loaf, and most of the basics like sugar, flour, and coffee were still attainable and reasonably priced. Because of the rapidly declining economy the average worker's income in the early 1930s had fallen to about thirty dollars per week.

The American dream, the great land of opportunity, had in the blink of an eye turned into a nightmare of what appeared to be the failure of capitalism. With the near collapse of the country's banking system and a definite lack of confidence in the unsteady economy during this deep depression, America, with all of its promises, had become a land of despair.

Despite the bleak times and the scarcity of money the Silvas survived because of John's steady hard work and Marta's ability to scrimp and save, and her natural knack at cooking simple but filling meals. Old country Portuguese linguica sausage, spicy soups, thick vegetable stews, and fresh yellow breads were a large mainstay of their meals. Like many immigrants they remained a strong, dedicated couple and had accepted the conditions of their hard times.

Life went on in their uncertain world, the Silvas and just about every other family living on the continent surviving on the brink of disaster. Even though day to day living was a strain there were some good times, and over the next few years little Johnny was blessed with a brother and then new twins, a baby sister and another brother.

Just as the Silva family was getting larger and stronger so was the country slowly moving toward its own recovery. By 1932 the government had established the Works Progress Administration which employed millions of men across the nation to work on building and improving highways, bridges, airports, and dams. Through these aggressive government work programs workers were paid only forty-one dollars a month, but they were glad to have the work and the income, no matter how meager.

Other relief programs, federally backed banking guarantees, massive public works projects, long term assistance programs, and safety net assurances initiated by the country's central government pushed through by the newly elected FDR administration, began turning the bleak economy around.

Without a doubt those who had lived through the precarious times of the Great Depression were most assuredly scarred by it. Their experiences of struggling and going without would remain with them throughout their lives.

As an infant, then later as a young boy, Johnny Silva had innocently observed and unmistakably absorbed the long-lasting effects of being poor and dependent. But, because of his parents, particularly his father, he was still a lucky little son, even despite his birth date.

When Johnny was about six years old, one day after returning home from work his father sat with him in their small, dark parlor on the third floor of their fourteen-dollar a month apartment. John senior thought it was about time to explain some important facts of life to his son. Back then, though family was foremost, men typically focused most of their attention on making a living. When it came to the kids, the father's responsibility was to keep them straight, usually with the wide end of a leather belt. It was the mother's job to rear the children.

John Silva was different. As a young boy he had been taught by his father, and his father's father. Although he had grown up in the old country and knew his place in this new world, he wanted to make sure his children learned from his own experiences. He wanted them to have a more promising life, an easier path then he had. Even at such an early age it was time for a father-to-son talk.

"Johnny come here," Mr. Silva called out when he arrived home from a long, raw-to-the-bone, cold day in the butcher shop. Johnny thought for certain he was in trouble and was afraid of getting a whipping. Maybe his father had found out he was out of line in school. The first grade was a tough adjustment for a six-year old kid. But how did his father know? The boy wondered.

Young Johnny held back in the bedroom he shared with his younger brother Barry, pretending not to hear his father. The infant twins, Donnie and Loran, were sleeping in the tiny closet-like room next to their parent's bedroom.

"Johnny, I want see you now," echoed the strong accented voice a second time. Knowing what might happen if he didn't go to his father, he slowly moved through the hall to where his dad was waiting.

"I called you boy. You no hear me calling you?"

"Yes sir," is all he could mumble, expecting the worst. He was ready to take his punishment and promised himself not to cry this time.

"Sit down son. I want talk to you," John senior said in his broken English.

Johnny quickly sat down, his first thought was to protect his bottom, and his second was that maybe his dad had something for him. On rare occasions his father would bring home a handful of loose candy for his children. Either way the little boy was relieved.

"How old you now son?"

"Dad, you know I'm six, seven pretty soon," the boy cautiously smiled.

The father began. "You growing up now," he said, patting his son's thick head of black hair.

Johnny looked up at his father. He admired the man, though this was the first time they had ever sat down together to talk.

"How you do in school?"

Oh, oh! Johnny thought to himself. 'I'm in for it now,' was the only thing that went through his first grader mind.

"Ah...good," he said, hesitating. "We're learning arithmetic," he volunteered, hoping his learning ability would weaken his dad's intent to reach for his belt.

"That good son. Keep up the good work. School important you know. You need do good in school and learn."

"Yes sir."

John senior added, "You little man now, you know that?"

"Yes sir," Johnny answered, brightening up a bit but still waiting for the belt to be pulled out of his father's trousers at any second. Misbehaving at school wasn't worth this, but sometimes Johnny just couldn't help himself.

"You know what being rich is?" his father asked him in all seriousness.

It was a grown-up question, but Johnny knew. "It's money, right?" he said, eager to impress his father.

"Yes, money, and lot more."

Even at almost seven years old, little Johnny had a sense of money. Every Saturday morning his mother gave him a nickel for doing various chores around the house. Taking out the rubbish, keeping his and his brothers' room clean, helping hang the laundry on the back balcony. These were things a youngster could do to earn a little change. He would typically take his allowance and buy some colored marbles or aggies, and a bag of candy bits. If he saved up enough maybe once a month he would take the electric trolley car to the movie house down in Porter Square and watch a matinee double feature with a couple of school chums and still have some pennies left over for popcorn.

His father continued. "We a lucky family, you know. We not rich, but we wealthy in things that important."

Johnny looked at his father with a confused frown on his dimpled face. It didn't seem that earning a nickel a week was being wealthy. Twenty-five cents a week would be wealthy, he thought to himself.

"I thought we were poor," the boy replied.

"Why you say that?" Mr. Silva asked his son.

"Some of the kids in school said it. They said we were poor and should go back to where we came from," Johnny answered.

John remembered when he was a child. "Kids can be mean. No pay attention to them Johnny. True, we don't have much money, but we live well. I have good job and your mama works hard taking care of you and your brothers and sister."

Little Johnny knew that much.

"We rich in different ways," his dad went on. "We have a home. Your mama make good meals. We love each other. These the most important things in life," Johnny's dad explained in his best fractured English.

Johnny knew that much too.

"Let me tell you something," John said as he put his strong arm around his oldest son. "There three things you need to learn and remember in this life."

The boy focused on his dad. He starred at his father's unshaven face, his reddened cheeks, his disheveled Mediterranean hair, his tired eyes. To Johnny his dad was the smartest man in the world.

Hoping his young son could understand what he was about to teach him, John Silva began. "Before your mama and me come to America I read as much I can about this great country. I want to learn the language. I want to know what make it so good here. I ask myself why everyone want to come here? Why people want to leave their homeland, their families and friends, come to a strange place, to learn a new language? I always wondered that."

He looked down at his boy to see if Johnny understood what he was trying to say. The little man nodded his shaggy head, not really knowing any of the answers, but trying to please his dad just the same.

"I read about early American history. I read how this country grow to become a great nation. I read everything about America. You ask your mama. I always have book with me. I read the words of many American writers and I want to learn what make this country work. And you know what?" he asked Johnny.

Johnny was still paying attention. "What Dad?"

"I find out what it is," John Silva said, as if he had discovered the secret of life. Deep inside he believed he had.

"Tell me," Johnny grinned, his sweet boyish face revealed how happy he was just to be with his dad, having a man-to-man talk, like two grown-ups, even though not everything his father said had registered.

John kept explaining, trying to talk in simple terms. "This a country of hard workers, of people wanting to learn and get along with everyone, of risk takers and explorers. This a whole continent of people who love their freedom and stand by their principles of decency and what is right."

Johnny was squirming in his seat listening to his dad. But it was better than getting a whipping any day.

His father had more to say. "The people here make it great. People from all over the world come here to work together and raise their families and look for the best things in their life. America a god-worshipping country where people can believe whatever they want. I love my Portugal, but this our home now. We know times are tough, for all of us, it will get better. This is a country of people who believe in themselves and are wanting to sacrifice to make a good life."

Johnny was showing his youthful impatience, but he remembered his dad had said there were three things he needed to learn. "What are the three things?" he asked his father.

His father hadn't forgotten.

"Free will," John held up one finger. "People here can be whatever they want. They can be butcher or teacher or businessman. They can be rich or poor. They can be Catholic or Protestant or Jewish. They can even be president of the country. That something to be proud of," John lectured to his son.

Johnny had already figured it out that being rich was better than being poor. He didn't know he could be the president though.

"Self-determination," John senior said with difficulty while extending two fingers. "People can do what they want with their lives. They can learn and work hard. They can follow their goals and reach their dreams. They can be whatever they want to be. Just like you son. When you grow up you can do anything you want to do."

"Finally Johnny," John Silva was coming to his conclusion as he held up three fingers to emphasize his lesson, "rugged individualism." This was a tricky word for him, but he knew it was important. He had read about it in his books. "That the really hard one. Everyone want to succeed and live well. We all want nice things. We want our families to be safe and happy. But there always be troubles, problems to overcome. No matter what you do there will be difficult times, hard work, unsure decisions, bad people. There are always bad people.

Little Johnny was completely lost by now. He didn't really understand what his dad was talking about, but he saw the passion in his father's motions and heard the genuine excitement in his voice which, like osmosis, where being imbedded into the boy's impressionable brain.

John had a bit more to say. "Life is not easy, but nobody ever said it would be. People who are strong and rugged and really believe in themselves can make a very nice life here in America."

By now Johnny was more than ready to go out to play.

But John senior had one more piece of advice for his young son. "Remember this last thing I tell you, Johnny. Always treat people with respect. Deep down most everyone the same, so respect them and their ways. And take care of the people you love, because they the most important people in your life. You do these things my son, and as sure as God is in heaven, good things will always come to you."

Young Johnny rose from his seat and hugged his dad. Some of what he had just learned would stick and grow with him as he became an adult.

"Okay, now go wash your hands, your mama should have supper ready soon," John Silva said, feeling good about time well spent with his first born. He looked up as if he were gazing at the stars, the heavens where his own dad had resided for a long, long time. He prayed his son Johnny would grow up to be a good man too.

From author's book *Johnny's Fortune*

Why Goals?

For many people, goal setting is assumed to be a long, drawn out, complicated, almost foreign task. Hundreds of questions bombard them from every angle. "What are goals?" "Do I really need goals?" "Where do I start?" "How can I discover what I truly want?" "What's the difference between short and long term goals?" "What's really important to me?" "How can I change?" "What do I need to do to stay focused or committed?" "Where can I turn for help?" "How can I change my habits?" "What am I doing wrong?" "How can I become a better person?" "What is my true purpose in life?"

For others, having a desire to grow and achieve goal setting seems to be an impossible undertaking. Excuses and tendencies to procrastinate control their lives and stop them in their tracks before they even begin the journey to a more promising future. "It's too hard." "It takes too long." "I'm too busy right now." "I have young children." "It's not the right time." "Maybe tomorrow." "I'll work on it later." "I'm too tired." "I can't afford it." "I'm a perfectionist." "I need to do research first." "I don't feel inspired."

And for many, self-doubt, the lack of confidence, or a low self-esteem prevent them from ever taking that first productive step. "I never finished school." "I'm not good enough." "I don't deserve it." "I have no will power." "I'm unlucky." "I'm too old." "I'm too young." "I don't have the education." "I have disabilities." "There's no point." "I can't do it." "I'm afraid of failure."

It's no wonder a cloud of mystery hovers over the whole goal setting process. It's a tangled mess of 'How tos' and 'What ifs.' Except for the annual short-lived New Year's resolutions, the vast majority of people never try to reach their illusive goals. These popular resolutions, however, are usually pie-in-the-sky wishes, non-genuine goals. Nearly 45% of Americans make New Year's resolutions and fewer than 10% actually achieve them.

By the first week of February most every reveler with high hopes and grand wishes give up on their new 'goals' of losing weight, or quitting smoking, or making more money, or eliminating debt. The recurring question is always the same: "Why didn't it work this time?"

Setting goals only works when there is a concrete plan, a simple map, a blueprint of action. Goals must be written down, otherwise they are mere fantasies. They must be specific, if not, they are unclear and ambiguous. They need to be measurable in manageable increments to validate success. They need to be rewarding to ensure continued accomplishments. They need to be challenging, but attainable through work and commitment. They must have a definite time frame, because deadlines force results.

Goals need to be important to the achiever, almost inspirational, to surmount the inevitable obstacles and difficult times. They must be visual and in-your-face as a daily reminder. And goals need to be shared with a strong support system of people who offer continued encouragement and peer pressure.

In this column we will take a step-by-step process in discussing both the mechanical 'nuts & bolts' and the human motivational behaviors behind successful goal setting leading toward magical results. We will look into the newest and most comprehensive goal setting model, known as SMART-ROADS, which covers all aspects of planned human achievement.

We will review the top reasons why goals are important and how to analyze different types of goals. We will identify essential goals in your lives and recognize how to accept them and commit to them. We will spend time learning how to eliminate bad habits and create positive new ones. In our pursuit of developing more productive, happier, and balanced lives, we will identify common mistakes in goal setting.

But most importantly, the goal of this writer is to show you the reader how to live a more enriching life and discover your true purpose. Goal setting done simply and properly can change your life.

It all begins with that first step.

From author's column in *The Sierra Vista Herald*

CHOICES

A thirty-five year old man decides to celebrate his job promotion with a group of buddies from work. By the time he's ready to head home it's past two in the morning and he is drunk. Despite what his friends say he insists on driving home. Just as he makes a wide turn into his darkened driveway a police car pulls him over. He is arrested for DUI and held in the local jail for the rest of the night. He pays exorbitant fines at his court hearing and loses his driver's license for six months. His neighbors saw the commotion outside his house and his wife is extremely angry with him. His two young children ask, "What happened to daddy?" The next day at work after the news spread, he is fired from his new Safety Officer position.

All because of choices.

Jason was a popular, energetic high school senior. He was ranked the highest scoring player in the region, carrying his team and school to record breaking victories. Because of his talent he had earned a full ride four-year scholarship at a prestigious northeastern university. It was his dream of a lifetime. His focus on sports hindered his academic grades, which were often overlooked due to his athleticism. Months before high school graduation he was caught cheating on his college entrance exams. It was the only way he could pass them, he figured. Besides, it was no big deal. He had gotten away with cheating in class many times before. A week later he received a letter rescinding his scholarship.

All because of choices.

A single mother struggles to pay her rent and care for her ten-year old daughter. She didn't finish high school and dropped out of GED classes. She was too busy and too tired from working full time as a waitress and four nights a week as a hotel clerk. Something had to change in her life. She had just turned twenty-seven and knew if she didn't do something about her situation she would be stuck forever. A friend told her about a two year nursing program at the nearby community college. Class times were flexible and costs for the program could be paid through grants if she earned her GED. After nearly twenty months of juggling bills, her studies, and caring for her child, she was offered a nursing job upon graduation.

All because of choices.

A young soldier listens to his uncle and takes his advice to buy a U.S. savings bond every month. An eighteen year old kid sees no reason to save for so far in the future. It's hard enough to get by with the meager pay he earns as a new recruit. But he takes his uncle's recommendation to heart and after being discharged four years later finds it was good guidance. Using them as collateral, the cash value of his accumulated bonds allowed him to buy his first new car. Shortly after, the savings was there for him and his young family to put down on the purchase of an inexpensive home. And from that small savings put aside each month, the road to moderate wealth had been paved.

All because of choices.

Will and Shirley are in there mid-50s. They had both worked their entire lives, and like most people, were overwhelmed with steady monthly bills. They had a pricey mortgage, two car payments, and too many high interest credit card bills. The years passed quickly and they were getting concerned for their retirement years. Spending more time with their grown children and grandchildren were important to them. Traveling the country and maybe taking in a cruise were in their future plans. So they hoped. But expenses had to be cut and savings had to be increased if they truly expected comfortable golden years. So they set strict monthly budgets, cut back expenses as best they could, and laid out a long-term financial plan as preparation for their senior days ahead.

All because of choices.

Betty, a middle aged mom, had neglected her health over the years, as many do. Between work and taking care of her family and keeping the house clean she was exhausted and had gained extra weight. Of course she wanted to live a healthy life style, but being so busy she depended on fast food meals and take-out orders, quick snacks and sodas throughout the day. One day, unable to fit into an old dress she wanted to wear to her friend's party she decided to do something. She began an exercise program, slow at first, then gradually intensified. She paid attention to what she and her family ate, making time to shop for more nutritious foods, many of which were easy and quick to cook. In the long run it benefited her and her family.

All because of choices.

Betty's good friend, Amy, was also overweight. For most of the same reasons, she had simply let herself go. High blood pressure, mild diabetes, and a general sense of fatigue had invaded her life. These medical concerns often led to feelings of frustration, and more recently, to periods of depression, sadness, and frequent spurts of hopelessness. To cope with her despair Amy resorted to food as a crutch. Desserts, unhealthy snacks, high sugar drinks. Her increased consumption of harmful foods gave her temporary relief, but ultimately made her situation even worse.

All because of choices.

A fifty-nine year old man was diagnosed with stage 3 lung cancer and had undergone surgery. The procedure was partially successful, but the man would live his remaining days attached to an oxygen tank and limited to restricted movement. He had smoked cigarettes since he was a teenager, a span of more than forty years. He knew smoking was dangerous. The coughing, the congestion, the shortness of breath. Everyone told him so. It was even printed on the side of every cigarette pack. But he kept smoking. At first it was cool. Then it became a habit. And expensive. "Later," he answered when people asked him if he would ever stop smoking. "Someday," he frequently promised. But he never did.

All because of choices.

A young family decided it was time to have their own home. They had been renting for years and were limited to what they could do inside their apartment. Mortgage interest rates were favorable and owning a small home would actually be less expensive than renting. Plus, the pride of ownership, the investment aspect, and the freedom of having their own place were exactly what this family wanted. Up until this turn of events they had never really paid much attention to their credit rating. They spent all their paychecks every week. They were often late on payments. And a few times they wrote off debts they disagreed with. When they went to get pre-qualified for a home mortgage their past financial mistakes had caught up with them. Of course they were denied the loan.

All because of choices.

Daily Decisions

We all must face making decisions every day. Hundreds, maybe a thousand daily choices direct our lives. They determine where we are, where we are going, and where we end up. Some choices or decisions are easy. What should I eat for breakfast? Which shirt should I wear? Where do I buy gas? Other choices can be more difficult, more life altering. Where should I go to school? What type of career do I want? What kind of life partner am I looking for?

A typical day in many peoples' lives can be quickly described as followed:

Get up, go to work, come home, eat dinner, spend time with the family or friends, go to sleep. Simple day-in and day-out things to do. Not too complicated. Easy to follow. Established routines. Not many crucial decisions to make. Just life.

But if you really look at the tremendous numbers of options involved, it can be overwhelming. Stressful might be a better description. How do you know if your choices are right? How do you know if they are dreadfully wrong? What if you simply refuse to make a choice? What then?

Well, let's look at a typical daily routine where even more countless choices, decisions, and alternatives come into play.

Get up in the morning. Six-thirty or seven? Is that enough time to get ready? Maybe sleeping in is a better idea. After last night's late movie a little extra sleep can't hurt. Can it? Take an early shower or would it have been better taken before bedtime? What brand of soap is used? Shampoo too? The cheap stuff or good quality name brand? Is there really a big difference? Maybe. Maybe not. Toothpaste and shaving cream and hair products and makeup. What's the best for the best price? Is the best affordable? Is it really worth it?

What's for breakfast? Eggs, hash browns, and bacon? Sounds good. Are there eggs in the fridge? Love bacon, but it's really not that good for the body. Maybe just a few pieces though. Cooking a full breakfast can take too long. Is there enough time? Maybe not. What about a bowl of cereal? Quick and easy. Which cereal? Is the milk still good? Rather have a donut. There's left-over pizza. Need coffee, that's for sure. With cream and sugar? Not too good either, but it tastes so good. Can't drink it black. Rather not have any. How about a nice cup of tea? Green, black, oolong, herbal, fermented, flavored? Too many choices. It's so confusing. Make it simple and pick up a Starbucks and scone on the way to work. But the cost adds up.

Now, what to wear to work? It's Monday, not Friday, so no casual wear. Long sleeve shirt, or short sleeve? It gets cold in the office. But I can wear my jacket. The blue one or the black one? Need to drop off my black jacket at the cleaners. Any tie should do. No one ever says anything about it at work. Shoes should be buffed up, but no time. Have to hit the road.

Monday morning traffic is terrible. Maybe calling in sick is a good idea. All my sick days have been used up already. And it's only May. Maybe try the back roads to work. But that's longer. Running low on gas. Should have gassed up yesterday. Hope there's enough to get there. Can't afford to be late...again. What if I get fired? Then what? Start all over again. That wouldn't be fun. Can't afford it either.

Stopping to pick up your coffee and breakfast roll takes longer than expected. Too many people had the same idea. Damn people. No cash in the wallet, so use the debit card. Haven't had cash in hand for a long time. Direct payroll deposit and plastic takes care of that. Drink coffee on the road and drop sticky crumbs on the blue jacket. The back roads are jammed with school buses, trash trucks, and delivery vans. Everyone looking for a shortcut. Gonna' be late.

At the office all the parking spots near the building are filled up. Have to park a block away. The boss is in his office so your tardiness isn't noticed. But the secretary is out front and she tends to squeal on people. The tight work cubicle desk is stacked with files that need immediate attention. Irate customers are calling looking for answers. Incoming emails are loading up the computer screen. And it's only 8:30.

The morning trails on as work is being completed slowly. The phone doesn't stop ringing and the PC messaging never ceases. Need to find another job. Less stressful, more money, maybe with a flexible work schedule. This job was supposed to be temporary, just a transition to something better. But so far that hasn't happened. Need to do something about that. When I have time. When I can afford the pay gap.

It's lunch time. A free hour. No phones. No emails. No interruptions. Quiet time. Same question as this morning. What to eat? How about in the cafeteria? Not too good. Same old food every day. Chicken, meatloaf, some sort of stir fry. Noisy dining area filled with people. Maybe hit the fast food joint across the street. A burger and fries and a soda. Had that the other day. Should have brought a salad or sandwich from home. Maybe tomorrow.

Clock back in. More of the same work. Your watch shows ninety minutes until break time. Finally five o'clock rolls around. Beat the rush home. But traffic is a caravan. Why's everyone heading in the same direction? Almost forgot, have to pick up a few things at the food market. Hot fried chicken or deli meats or something microwaveable. Keep it easy. Hope the old folks aren't there. Takes them forever to check out.

An hour later you arrive at your apartment and get to park two buildings away. Once inside, the dog reminds you he needs to be walked. Where's his damn leash? Oh yeah, he ate it last week. A belt works. He wants to run and play, but there's no time for it. Have to eat dinner then do some laundry. Maybe watch the tube for a while. Call some friends and make plans for Saturday. Restaurant or bar or party or movies? Whatever works. Come eleven at night you find yourself nodding off. Time to go to bed. Tomorrow is another day. Another day of the same old stuff. Same choices. Same decisions. Same results. Maybe it's time to do something different.

As you can see, there are hundreds of choices in front of you each and every day. The question is, 'Are you in control of your life or have you allowed other people and daily circumstances to control your time, your future, and your happiness?'

Take control. It's up to you.

21 Rules of Blackjack

Rule #1 Blackjack, also known as '21', is gambling.
Gambling is betting. Betting is risky.
CAUTION!
You can lose your money, but you can also win.
Don't be stupid. Learn the rules.

Rule #2 Don't play if you can't afford to lose. If you drink
and are comfortable playing $5 hands, don't try to
show off your champagne taste with $25 bets.

Rule #3 If other players at the table can't count to 21, get
up and leave. Refer to Rule #1.
Don't play with idiots. It will cost you.

Rule #4 Dealers don't really mean it when they wish you
'Good Luck.' However, when you are winning,
it's good practice to tip the dealer.

Rule #5 Always present your Player's Card to the dealer or
pit boss for points. Getting comps and free stuff is
always a good thing.

Rule #6 When possible, take position at third base, the seat
closest to the dealer's right, the last spot to be
dealt. BUT, you should know how to play well,
because the table is depending on you to make
good decisions.

Rule #7 Limit your buy-in. It's real money! Plastic is
easier to spend than crisp hard earned dollars.
Don't be tricked.

Rule #8 A standard deck of cards contains 52 cards, 4
         suites. You should know this, if not, you have no
         reason to be playing cards.

Rule #9 A common six deck shoe contains 312 cards, 24
         of each number (24 aces, kings, queens, etc.), 96
         ten value cards total.
         Again, basic blackjack knowledge.

Rule #10 Learn how to monitor card trending (counting
         cards.) Not that you could really count 6 decks,
         but there is something to be said about paying
         attention to the flow of cards and using it to your
         advantage.

Rule #11 Play conservatively at first with your chips, then
         more aggressively with winnings (house chips).
         Remember, doubling down is how to win money.

Rule #12 Never split 10s. Only morons split 10s, even
         against a dealer's bad card.

Rule #13 Never split an Ace-ten blackjack. Yup, people
         actually do that when the payout on a blackjack is
         low. Still a stupid move in my opinion. Plus, you
         probably will piss off the other players.

Rule #14 Always split 8s and aces. Duh! Basic strategy. If
         you don't do this, go back to the slots.

Rule #15 The ability to 'surrender' half your bet can be a
         good tactic. This can save you on a really bad
         hand, however, few casinos allow it. You can
         figure out why.

Rule #16 Side bets can be fun and profitable. Dealer match, dealer push, and other side bets make the game more interesting. Put a dollar on the side.

Rule #17 Spanish blackjack offers more ways to win. More options offer more challenges. Also, there are no 'ten' cards in the deck, which tends to favor the house odds.

Rule #18 Don't dig in your wallet or purse for more cash or hit the ATM to chase your loses. If you're on a losing streak (it does happen), then step away for a while.

Rule #19 Slow down your play when one-on-one with the dealer. Some dealers like to fast deal. More hands give the house an advantage. Order a drink, go to the restroom, make unhurried decisions. Slow the dealer down.

Rule #20 Don't bet stupid. This can't be emphasized enough. Blackjack is a game of chance where the odds are fair to the player, but it should always be viewed as a means of entertainment. Keep your day job!

Rule #21 Be self-disciplined and leave a winner. If you are up a bit, learn to walk away. It is easy to win, but difficult to walk away from the action.

Release Their Potential

A nation's future lies with its youth. Our younger generation's future relies on its education. Their education is our responsibility. We must be accountable for our children's success, well-being, innovation, and prosperity. We either help them to succeed or show them how to fail. Something needs to be done.

There are approximately 56.6 million elementary and secondary students in public, charter, and private schools in America. Sixteen million students attend our colleges and universities. Seventy-three million young minds are at stake, screaming for help, looking for direction, ready to take on the world if they were only given the right tools.

Every student, every adult, everyone in the world wants a good life. Education and training and mentoring and caring and guidance are the keys toward achieving that good life. We as responsible adults, parents, and educators must step up to ensure these methods of knowledge are passed on.

1.2 million high school students drop out of school each year. That's 7,000 students giving up every day! One quarter of all freshmen do not graduate from high school on time. The drop-out rate for first year college students is unacceptable. Clearly, many of our institutions of learning can be labeled as 'drop-out factories' leading to widespread financial insecurities, increased crime, and a tremendous loss of productivity and personal potential.

'What if...' we could release the full pent-up potential of our youth? What kind of scientific or medical or inventive breakthroughs could be discovered? What unknown innovations could be put into place? What types of advances could be developed to improve the human condition? These are questions often not addressed.

My suggestion is to "Do Something!" In my opinion two aspects of education, whether from our schools or from within the family unit, are terribly lacking.

The first is goal setting. Every one, students in particular, should learn effective principles of setting goals in their personal, academic, and later, their professional lives. Plans at each phase of their lives should be established and followed through to the desired results.

Second is the lack of strong soft skills, commonly referred to as 'people skills.' Strong soft skills, specific personal characteristics and traits, are essential to one's success. The three skills most lacking in today's workplace are Communication, Critical Thinking, and Interpersonal Skills. These can be taught and improve upon to unleash unlimited potential.

I think it's time to "Do Something!" about this before it's too late.

From a March 2019 Linked-in post by the author

Always 100%

Not too long ago I was a college instructor teaching English to adult foreign students. Morning and evening classes, three days a week with some of the most amazing people I have ever known. They came from countries all around the world and spoke many different languages. Their lives were diverse in education level, culture, age, background, and opportunity. But every one of them wanted the same thing. They wanted to learn English as a first step toward reaching the American dream.

It was my job to help them.

I was once asked by the program director what percentage of my students did I expect to show an educational gain during the current semester. According to Arizona state standards each class was expected to show a seventy percent gain rate in student learning. This from bureaucrats who had never set foot in front of a class room, who had never held the future of students in their hands.

So, I surmised, according to the guidelines seven out of ten students where to show marked improvement in their English language skills over an eight week period. What about the other students? I thought. What about the three who didn't show ed-gains on convoluted, ambiguous, and biased listening, speaking, reading, and writing tests?

What would happen to them?

As instructors were we to give up on the lower thirty percent? Were we to concentrate on the 'smarter' students and let the others go by the wayside? Falter through class? Give up through desperation? Drop out and except less in life?

I couldn't live with that.

If I believed in this defeatist principle I would naturally have to accept the assumed fact that not every student could meet the mark. I'd have to accept the idea that some students simply could not learn.

I knew every one of my students. I knew their struggles and concerns. I knew their strengths and weaknesses. I knew their wants and desires and dreams. Each one of them deserved a full and equitable chance, provided they committed.

If I believed in the mandated numbers passed down, I had a major problem. I had pressing questions:

"Which three would I let go?"

"Which thirty percent would I write off?"

The answer was simple.

Not a one.

Answering my director's question about what percentage of my students I expected to show gain, I said, "100%. I always expect every student to learn."

By the way, I no longer teach there.

From author's post on Linked-in

D.O.M.
Dangerous Old Men

They were heading into the valley of unknown. From the low rocky ridge he peered into the arid basin bordered by the Spring Mountains. The lifeless range ran north to west as a natural barrier. He looked down at the small, fenced camp. It was no larger than a forty acre parcel of desert hidden in the open. At first glance he could see no activity through his powerful binoculars. Something strange had happened. He adjusted the dial and focused in closer on the closed front gate.

"Two guards," he said. "Both of them appear to be down."

"Maybe our plan worked," another member of the team remarked.

"Not so fast," Michael cautioned. "Who usually gets guard duty?"

The man riding gunshot quickly answered. "New recruits and fuck-ups."

"Exactly."

They drove faster toward the compound, kicking up a cloud of fine dust as they sped through the sparse Nevada desert. All five men in the rented jeep remained quiet, in their minds reviewing the mission. Going through practiced details. Anticipating the worst. Prepared for a lethal encounter. But in truth, they really weren't well prepared. Not nearly as prepared as they should have been. In the next minute they could be killed.

One of the team in the back seat, concern in his voice, said, "This is crazy. Between us we have three ancient pee-shooters from a pawn shop and a damn knife. What the hell are we gonna do if they're ready for us?" He wasn't really worried. Just stating facts.

"They won't be," the leader assured.

"But what if it didn't work?"

"Trust me. It worked," Michael said in a confident tone. In all of their encounters he had never steered his crew wrong.

Ten minutes later they pulled up in front of the double gate. The April sun was high creating tight, contained shadows. The gate was secured with a chain padlocked from inside. Sure enough both guards were slumped on the ground. No resistance. Not yet.

No sounds came from inside the encampment.

That was a good sign. Maybe the plan actually worked.

The men jumped out of the jeep. Without a word Pitts drew his antique pistol and shot the lock off the chain. The links fell loose and he kicked open the gate. One guard, dressed in a dirty camouflaged uniform was flopped over, his rifle dropped in the dirt to his side. He was definitely dead. The other guard, a younger man, was still alive, but barely. He looked up at the foreigners entering his post. His eyes were wide and glassy filled with mixed fear and hope. His mouth and beard dribbled with yellow saliva. A bubbling foam oozed from his dried lips. The boy soldier reached his hand out to the rescuers as best he could. Confused and scared and hurt he searched for help. His mouth moved slightly, quivering. "Wa...wa..." he tried to say in vain.

"Water? You want water?" Pitts asked in anger. He looked at the savage, pure fury in his eyes. He lowered his pistol, jabbed the barrel into the soldier and shot him in his forehead.

"Was that really necessary?" the team leader asked.

"What the fuck!" Pitts, the ex-New York cop who in his life had seen too much death and destruction, said with unmitigated wrath in his expression. "You know what they did." Forgiveness was not one of his redeeming qualities when it came to these people. They had caused enough death and pain and suffering. Pitts had seen too much of it. This was the beginning of their demise as far as he was concerned. "Besides, he was already dead."

The men cautiously entered the compound, eyes searching, moving in short strides, those with weapons at the ready. Michael, still called Sarge by his men, quickly commanded, "FB, Sergio, take the right flank. Sandy and Pitts, go left." The men moved instinctively, waiting for anything to happen.

Pitts' gunshot had certainly announced their arrival. Return gun fire was expected at any instant. But the camp stayed quiet. To the right were the terrorists' trucks neatly backed into their places. Two well-maintained army issue troop carriers with canvas tarps covering their backs. Three Ford extended cargo vans with Nevada plates. Next to the vehicles were rows of rough-hewn wooden picnic tables with attached wooden bench seats. Ten of them neatly lined up. A large netted camouflaged cover held up by wood posts offered some relief from the desert sun. An open communal dining area for the troops. Farther down the line were several storage sheds. Two eight by eight wooden structures and one twice that size. Then smaller shacks. Near the rear of the camp was a short makeshift firing range set up for pistol practice. Adjacent to that stood a twelve-foot tall above-ground metal water tank with a plastic pipe running down its side, capped with a spigot valve.

Along the southern perimeter was a weathered twenty-by-twenty foot square structure, most likely the camp commander's quarters. A crude handwritten sign not in English identified the building's occupant. Functional and private for the man in charge. Beyond that was a long single story barracks-type building large enough to quarter the fifty soldiers supposedly stationed there. It looked like the old World War II clapboard quarters built for American soldiers in training throughout the country. Farther down the perimeter was a line of common latrines open to the elements.

The camp was much like the team had seen a day earlier in their recon trip. Only this time in more detail. The five ex-soldiers stealthily moved along the inner boundary fencing. No action, yet. Still quiet, but the scene before them was unmistakable.

Where was the return fire?

Where were the murderers?

Seconds into the raid the team found what they had hoped to find. A dozen or so militants dressed in their green-brown combat fatigues where strewn throughout the desert camp. They lie still on the picnic tables as if they had grown tired and suddenly feel fast asleep. As if they had no time or energy to move. Half consumed food on thin tin plates was scattered on the tables. Some found its way to the ground. Some plates were flipped upside down. Plastic cups of drinks were in disarray. Several were half full. Most were toppled on the tables. A few had rolled off the planks.

Several of the residents were awkwardly folded backwards over their benches, their legs wedged beneath the planked seats preventing them from hitting the packed earth. Some lay face down, still heaving and sucking for air. Wheezing in blowing sand and desperately gasping their final breaths of life. Others on the dirt floor lay still. They had the same disgusting yellow slime leaking from their mouths as the dead guards. Like sleeping men drugged and downed almost instantly. More dead mercenaries throughout the compound convulsed in violent seizures, having no idea what had happened to them. Grabbing their throats and hacking their lungs out in a frightening attempt to rid themselves of something evil that had overcome them.

The patriots scanned the grounds for active survivors. The plan had worked but survivors could still be dangerous.

Filled with contempt and raw hatred, Pitts and FB, with no hint of mercy for the bastards, hurriedly shot those still moving. Between twenty and thirty military combatants were already dead, tortured anguish and twisted horror frozen on their filthy bearded faces. They had finally gone to see their maker and the promised seventy-two virgins.

Good luck to them.

"Behind you!" Sandy yelled at Sergio as they shifted through the stark barracks stacked with rows of tiered beds and battered foot lockers.

Without hesitation Sergio twisted around, and with his pee-shooter blasted the soldier in the chest who had wildly aimed his AK-74 machine gun at the intruders. The dead man fell backward into the building like a rubbery rag doll, knocking over bed frames and racks of uniforms.

"Thanks, buddy," Sergio said. "I owe you one."

"I shouldn't have to remind you, but you owe me more than one."

Immediately another warrior rushed in to kill the infidels. Sandy, the old surfer dude who had no gun, swiftly unsheathed his cherished KA-BAR combat knife and flipped it precisely into the on-comer's straggly neck. A guttural sound was the last utterance from the doomed soldier as his hands grasped his fatal wound.

The two men smiled at each other.

Just like old times.

The entire team searched the forty-acre compound for more live threats. They were quick and precise and thorough. Having found none, they let their guard down ready to call an all clear. Suddenly a terrorist emerged from one of the deuce-and-half trucks backed against the fence. He seemed deranged and apparently out of his mind. His movements were erratic. No visible gun in hand. No knife, no rifle. No weapon at all. He just ran toward the unit members screaming, "Allahu Akbar, Allahu Akbar!" his hands flailing high above his head as if he were calling for the wraith of his god on his enemies.

The men found cover, Pitts and FB and Sergio quickly taking aim before the radical terrorist pulled a pin from a grenade in his clenched hand. In three short seconds he blew himself up, his body parts scattered in the middle of the camp as the explosion echoed in the wind.

"Good fuckin' riddance!" Pitts said with conviction. "Saved me the damn trouble."

"That's what these people do," Sandy said.

"What?" someone asked.

"Blow themselves up for the glory of their cause."

"Okay men, ten minutes, max. Let's move it," Sarge reminded them of their tight time schedule.

They continued to comb the camp, checking the other trucks, the latrine, the out-buildings, the fence perimeter. But no one else was left alive. An unexpected strong desert wind swept through the compound laying heated dust on everything in the open like an old, abandoned ghost town left to indifferent elements of dust and wind and sun. What a miserable place to be. Why in the hell were these people here, each of the men wondered.

Sandy and Sergio completed their rounds. "Looks like the body count is forty-seven total," Sergio reported to Sarge.

"Sounds about right," he answered, recalling the small number marked on the map next to each of the terrorist camp sites. Fairly accurate FBI estimates of manpower. Good to know.

"We have a situation," FB, the retired vet and Chicago cop rushed forward and interrupted the men.

"What is it?" Sarge asked.

"Last we saw, there were four white Ford cargo vans next to the deuce and halves," FB said.

"Yeah."

"Well, there are only three. One's missing."

"Then we need to hurry," Sarge repeated. Loose ends. There were always loose ends in any mission. And they could cause serious problems.

They hastily searched the sheds for hidden equipment, weapons, and stragglers attempting to hide themselves from the slaughter. In one small shack they found a gas generator and several ten-gallon propane tanks. Another contained boxes of canned and dried food supplies. Even stacks of MREs, military issued meals ready to eat. Army surplus, no doubt. Good enough for our men, good enough for our enemies. In a large outbuilding next to the barracks the men did find something amazing.

"Sarge," Sandy hollered. "Check this out."

Hundreds of new assault rifles, all cleaned and ready for use, were neatly packed in crates. They had foreign markings stamped on the outside. Boxes of extra ammo lay next to the rifles. Enough to sustain a small army in a lengthy encounter. It was Russian weaponry identified by the Cyrillic script. Two cases of new generation M67 grenades with English markings were in the shed as well. US Army issue. Next to them were two long reinforced crates packed with powerful Swedish AT-4 rocket launchers. Hand-held widow makers designed for urban warfare. Additional rockets were sealed in more crates.

"Holy Shit!" Pitts groaned.

"These bastards were ready for some serious business," FB added. "How in the hell did they get their filthy hands on this kind of armory?"

"Top grade weapons," Sergio added. "Hard to come by."

Sarge glanced at his team. He had no answer. All he knew was that it took money to run a war. And with the right amount of cash, anything was available. "Put them in a van, we'll take them. Get the assault rifles from the dead too. We may be able to use them."

The men grinned. For the moment it didn't matter how and from where these weapons were acquired.

Excellent move.

"Sandy, find the keys to one of the vans. I want to head out in under five minutes," Sarge ordered, checking his watch.

"Where are we going to put all this stuff?" Sandy asked, and then too late decided it was a stupid question.

"We'll figure it out when we get back to town," Sarge said.

Sarge had a thought. "Sandy, you, Pitts, and FB, just before we high tail it out of here, toss some of those grenades in strategic spots. Storage sheds, barracks, the army trucks too. No need to leave evidence or valuable equipment for the other bad guys who are certain to find out what had happened here."

"Got it Sarge," Sandy acknowledged.

"We'll level the goddamn place," FB added.

Sarge and Sergio opened the door to the commander's quarters while the other men loaded the van. A small, thin soldier was sitting at his desk. He was bent over as if he were resting his head on his desk for a few minutes. In full uniform with strange insignia he must have been the compound commander. He was dead like the rest of his men.

"Check everything," Sarge said. "We might find something useful." Sarge saw the dead man's handgun and removed it from his holster. He slipped it in the front of his belt. It felt good to have a real weapon with him.

They kicked over piles of boxes. Inside were nothing but discolored papers, three-holed manual covers, and old files still in their green hanging sleeves. Too much to look through now and too much to carry with them. This stuff had been there for a long time. Sergio kicked through the papers. And lo and behold! He uncovered a stack of dog-eared copies of Playboy with their high-quality colorful airbrushed beauties seductively calling every man's ego. There was at least several years' worth.

Sergio picked up the top copy and admired the bunny of the month. He opened it to the center and let it unfold. "Hey Sarge," he said pointing to the three-page glossy center. "Miss January, 2018. This guy had something right."

Sergio tossed the magazine aside, turned and opened the top drawer of a single file cabinet against the wall. A long row of orderly files filled the space. Each one was labeled in a strange script. He opened a few of the files. They contained typed sheets of paper, maps of city streets, structure layouts, topographic maps, engineering designs, blueprints and schematics. They were stuffed with black and white matted eight-by-ten photos. Most were exterior shots, up close and from afar, from every conceivable angle. But many were obviously taken from within the buildings, which promised to be even more ominous. He opened the lower three drawers, all of which were similarly packed.

"Ah...Sarge. You should see this."

"In a minute," Sarge answered as he rummaged through the camp commander's desk. It was one of those old boxy, gray steel desks found in every military office. Solid enough to last another fifty years. In the top drawer he found nothing of value. Pens and pencils, yellow highlighters, staples, paper clips, scissors, colored sticky notes, and tattered business cards. Typical office supplies found in every desk. The middle drawer was empty except for extra ammo for the sidearm. Sarge pocketed it.

Then he tried the bottom drawer. It was locked. He kicked it a couple times without success. No time to waste he pulled the newly acquired pistol and shot the lock. The unexpected blast scared the hell out of Sergio. "Sorry about that," Sarge half apologized.

Inside the drawer was a closed cardboard container the size of a shoebox. He opened the lid carefully. A huge grin crossed his face. Christmas time in April. The box was stuffed with bundles of cash wrapped in bank paper bands, each marked $5000. He flipped through the packs. American hundred dollar bills. All crisp and new and unused and tightly packed.

Sergio saw the stash as Sarge removed the box. He let out a long whistle. "Must be fifty-thousand bucks there! What the hell? They must have had something serious planned."

"Closer to a hundred grand," Sarge said as he did a quick unofficial count.

"What do you think it's for?" Sergio wondered out loud. "Payroll?"

Sarge shook his head. "These guys probably don't get paid."

"For more equipment?"

"They look pretty well set," Sarge commented, his mind rushing over the possibilities, none of which were good.

"Maybe it's payoff money."

"Could be. But it doesn't really matter now. Does it?" Sarge said. "It's ours now," he added, closing the top and picking up the box. "Spoils of war."

Sergio, an eighth generation Texas rancher and also an arms expert with years of warfare experience both in Nam and the Middle East and along the southern most Mexican-American border, moved to the desk and shuffled through the paperwork and documents while Sarge continued his search.

He stopped in his tracks. "Oh hell Sarge!"

"What do you have?"

Sergio opened a bound folder paper-clipped with a photo of one of the greatest structures ever built in America. He spread the papers from inside the file flat on the desk around the dead guy. Highlighted areas marked ingress/egress locations. Penetration points were clearly identified. Security sentry positions coded in different shades. Also, many yellow colored explosive sites dotted the diagrams at key sites.

"Oh hell is right!" Sarge agreed, reviewing the photo.

They stared at the sophisticated exterior and interior drawings. They were detailed designs of the Hoover Dam located sixty miles from Las Vegas, a hundred miles from the terrorist camp they had just put out of commission. The words were foreign but the intent was clearly understood. It was a target.

"This is bad," Sarge said. "Real bad."

Sergio nodded. A terrorist attack on the Hoover Dam would be catastrophic, causing appalling destruction down the Black Canyon region and farther downstream. Hydro-electrical production would come to a shrieking halt affecting over eight million people in Arizona, California, and Nevada. Las Vegas and other cities would go dark in minutes. The five-hundred foot deep Lake Mead fed by the mighty Colorado River would dump trillions of gallons of water downstream. Regional agricultural irrigation would cease. Smaller towns and cities in its path would be wiped out. The steady supply of potable water for larger southwestern population centers would end. The regional and national economies would collapse from the disaster. It would take decades to rebuild.

Back before World War II, in 1939, Nazi agents attempted to blow up the dam to shut down the new electric grid. Their main mission was to hinder the developing aviation manufacturing industry in southern California. Fortunately, the bold plan was discovered and stopped before any damage was done. Today, most vehicle traffic bypasses the dam roadway and travels a newer nearby highway as a precautionary step to thwart further terrorist sabotage. But in today's world of terror, there was always someone trying their best to destroy America.

The men found a single typed sheet of paper that stood out from the rest. It was a lengthy list of possible nearby targets with English translations next to each site. Someone had begun checking off the locations. Addresses and coordinates identified their positions. They included what were referred to as soft, vulnerable targets like city shopping malls, professional sporting events, local movie theaters, community colleges, neighborhood libraries, regional hospitals and chain restaurants. All well-populated ordinary places scattered within the city of Las Vegas limits. All filled with people effortlessly hit.

Easy targets.

Prime terrorists marks.

Perfect kill zones with high potential body counts and chaotic impact.

Attacks of any kind in such places would cause utter pandemonium in the city and throughout the country. Unbounded panic would follow. Fear would take over. Businesses would shut down. All commerce would stop. Law enforcement would be on high alert. U.S. soldiers and Army reserves would be deployed in a show of strength. City, state, and national leaders would try to ease the apprehension by declaring all was safe. But few would believe them.

Quickly glancing at the file, Sergio eyed one familiar location. It was at the center of Fremont Street, known as the Fremont Experience, not a hundred feet from their hotel. Right across the pedestrian street from where the men had their coffee and breakfast. It was too close to home, striking a raw nerve. "This is personal now," he said.

Then, on a second page was another list. These were the harder, more secure targets seemingly impossible to take down with their in-place systems of high-tech security. McCarran International Airport not far from The Strip. Nellis Air Force Base on the northern outskirts of town. The FBI building in North Las Vegas. Even the central Las

Vegas Metropolitan Police Station. These were serious take-down-the-government type assaults that would leave the metro area helpless. Hard-core objectives.

"We need to get these to someone. And soon," Sarge stated. He stuffed the documents inside his shirt.

Sergio agreed. "This is way above our heads."

"No shit!"

"What about the file cabinet?" Sergio asked.

"Leave them," Sarge said. "This should be enough."

As they began to exit the room they heard a tinny sound. It came from a bulky satellite phone vibrating on the desk just within reach of the dead man's hand. Sarge remembered there was no cellular phone service in this off-the-grid part of the desert. The phone chirped again.

"What do you think?" Sergio asked.

"Answer it," Sarge said, figuring what could they lose?

Sergio picked it up and punched a button on the phone. Immediately a loud voice filled the speaker. It was angry and imposing. Demanding and authoritative. It was in a foreign language. A deep guttural tone. Arabic, or maybe even Farsi. Though the two men were vaguely familiar with these languages from their tours of duty in the Middle East, they could not determine which.

The voice continued its tirade. Finally in frustration the caller switched to very passable English. "Ahmed, what is going on over there? We have been trying to contact you all this morning. What has happened? Why do you not answer us?"

Sergio looked at Sarge as if to say, "Should I answer?"

Sarge simply shrugged. Why not?

"Ah...Hola amigo. Who is calling please?"

"Who is this? Where is Ahmed? What has happened?" the caller insisted.

"Well," Sergio continued. "Ahmed and the rest of his buddies can't come to the phone right now. They're in a better place with all their butt-ugly girlfriends." Sergio was actually having fun even though this was serious business. He grinned at Sarge.

"What? Who is this? I insist. Who is this?" The voice rattled off in his native language, obviously confused, but pissed off to the hilt.

"You don't know us, amigo. But you're gonna find out. Real soon. But since you do insist, let me tell you. We are the ones who will take you and your dirty rotten scum out. You come into our country and threaten us? You dare to wreak terror and havoc here? You think you can get away with your terrorizing and killing of innocent Americans? Do you really believe you can show up in our own back yard and take over? Well, compadre, let me tell you something. You and yours are gonna wish you never stepped foot in my country. I promise you that."

Sarge smiled back at Sergio. Good job. Give him hell.

The irate voice ranted on, but Sergio interrupted.

"Oh…and to really answer your question. Who are we? We are the ones who will wipe you and your kind off the face of the earth. We are the demons in your dreams. The boogie men under your beds. The faces of doom you will fear to the end. We are the D.O.M.s. The Dangerous Old Men." Sergio smiled. "Adios amigo." And he shut the phone down.

"Let's get the hell out of here," Sarge said, grabbing the phone and box of cash as his men running through the death camp began blowing up every standing structure in the camp, including the poisoned water tank.

From author's Prologue of *D.O.M.*

Two Weeks' Notice

Robbie was ambitious. He lived for adventure. He liked taking risks. He had no problem going out on his own to make things happen. He was independent and completely self-reliant. He was also stubborn. Sometimes it was good. Other times it worked against him.

He didn't need help from other people because even at the young age of sixteen he had already learned that help rarely comes. He'd rather be left alone instead of being told what to do and how to do it. He would make mistakes, but that was okay. He would learn from them. When he had a good idea, he would simply pursue it. When he wanted to try something, whether dangerous or risky or seemingly foolish, he would do it. When he was tired of doing the same old thing, he would change it.

Robbie was his own man and he was determined to always stay that way. To some, that type of outlook would seem destructive. His apparent renegade attitude would get him nowhere in life, particularly when he grew old enough to get a job, perhaps even start a career. Employers liked people who were committed to their corporate mission. They wanted people who followed orders to better improve the company. They sought people who traded loyalty for salary and possible retirement in the distant future.

All fair and honest attributes from within, but Robbie thought differently. He had these commendable traits. He did have a sense of commitment toward what had to be done. But his commitment was to himself as he searched for what was best. He did work well with others to accomplish better results. However, he believed that being accountable to others was important, but being responsible to himself had priority. He did believe in being loyal, to a point. But he believed that loyalty began at home, and he would always stay loyal to himself and his strong principles.

When he was a sophomore in high school Robbie got a job at the local grocery store. Bagging groceries, stocking food shelves, cleaning refrigerator units. He was a good and conscientious employee. When his boss told him what needed to get done, he did it. And he always did extra work without being asked. When they were short of help, Robbie offered to work extra hours. When customers were cranky or the boss was in a bad mood or other kids working there were slacking off, Robbie went the extra step to make things right. It was all about attitude, and Robbie had a positive one.

But Robbie easily got bored doing the same thing over and over again. It's not that he didn't like his duties, he just wanted more. Something different. Something more challenging. More stimulating. Once he got the itch he looked beyond.

After graduating from high school he had no plans. College was out of the question. He had had enough of the classroom. Plus there was no money for higher education. The two most popular options were factory work in town or stay at the grocery store. Neither sounded too exciting. The war in Southeast Asian was raging on, so Robbie, like most of his buddies, signed up for the military.

Having some time before he was supposed to show up for basic training Robbie decided to have some fun first. He gave his boss at the store two weeks' notice, then headed to Las Vegas with his buddy John Longo. Longo had already joined the Marines and was flying out to San Diego. He first wanted to stop at his cousin's place in Vegas for a few days. He invited Robbie to tag along, so they went.

Four years in the military was a long time for a young man like Robbie. Again, he liked his work maintaining camera systems on Air Force fighter jets as they flew sorties day and night in the war effort. He was stationed at a central Thailand air base where there was lots of work and action. It was exciting work for a young man. Much better than making light fixtures in a factory or cleaning meat cases.

He married a beautiful Thai woman and they had a small bungalow on the outskirts of his base. Within a year the couple had a son and Robbie was allowed to extend his tour in country. However, the war was scaling back. Troops were being rotated back home. Other airmen in his unit were re-upping for another four years prior to returning to the states. With it came a hefty sign-up bonus of five thousand dollars. This was back in the early 1970s when five grand was a damn fortune. Close to two years pay for an E-4.

Robbie was offered the bonus if he tested out as an E-5 sergeant which he could have done easily. Before deciding, he stopped and looked around. He looked at his job which was close to being cut way back once the war ended. He looked at the 'lifers' in the unit. Many of them did little work. They walked around all day with a coffee cup in their hand. Most of them were divorced. More than half were alcoholics. It was a clear vision into the future.

He also looked at his friends who eagerly signed up for the bonus at the cost of four years of their lives. Some of them had ordered a new car for when they got home. It seemed a high expense to pay. Their bonus would be gone in no time and they would be stuck. They would be on track for twenty years in the service. They would be locked into monotonous days and weeks of routine training. They would be at the mercy of the government to be relocated anywhere and at any time.

Robbie had only two weeks remaining to take the sergeant's test and decide whether he wanted to sign up for the additional four years. He let the deadline go by without hesitation. He wanted to do what he wanted to do. He wanted his family to always be together. He wanted them to stay in one place where they could be comfortable and safe. He wanted his children to have their own rooms, to keep their friends, to know their mom and dad would always be there for them.

The five thousand dollar bonus would come in handy, but it didn't even come close to what his life was worth. Instead of signing up, Robbie moved on. Instead of taking the money, Robbie took the road. Instead of dedicating his life to a structured and controlled career, Robbie re-entered the civilian world where opportunities abounded. He had absolutely no idea of what he was going to do. And he was okay with that.

Needing to earn a living Robbie got a job at a factory in town. He worked at the end of a long manufacturing line. His job was packing the many types of florescent lighting units after they were assembled. It was monotonous work. The only thing that changed was the size of the boxes. The morning shift buzzer started the lines and the afternoon end-of-shift buzzer shut them down. When overtime was offered, Robbie took it. When Saturday work was available, Robbie took it. Every payday Robbie thought about that five-thousand dollar bonus that he blew off. But he kept working.

He had to do something with his life. It was time. With his VA education benefits he decided to go to school. The only way to get his degree, he figured, was to attend college full time. It would take forever going part time and working a full time job. So he enrolled and gave his two weeks' notice to his factory supervisor. It was time to get ready for the rest of his life.

While studying at the university he got a part-time night job at UPS unloading and loading packages on trucks. It was good work. Good exercise and pretty good pay. His days were busy, but he was inching toward a better life. In time he became the shift supervisor. The position had merit. Robbie envisioned a possible promising career. He worked hard. He was conscientious about performing his duties. When he had graduated from school and wanted more, perhaps, he thought, it was the right time to settle down in a legitimate position with an establishment company.

Approaching his thirtieth birthday Robbie met with his depot manager. He asked if he could move into a full time higher management position within the company. He asked if it was possible for him to earn $50,000 a year, a very comfortable income for 1980. He was assured of a near future promotion. He was also told, of course, he could earn a very solid salary, but travel and relocating would most likely come with the new job. He was informed that a decision would be made within a couple weeks and he would be notified.

Robbie was fine with that. The wheels were beginning to turn. In his mind he was making plans, preparing for the move. Every day he waited for word from his manager. Every day he heard nothing. Finally, at the end of two weeks he asked about the new position. "Haven't heard anything yet," the manager said.

Somewhat disappointed, but still determined, Robbie told his boss, "I've enjoyed working here and I appreciate your efforts to help me move up in this company. But two weeks have come and gone. So as of today, I am giving you my two weeks' notice." And he walked out of the office, wondering what the hell was next.

He and his family then moved to Arizona. He was searching for opportunities. He wanted to work for himself. He wanted to make things happen. He wanted to survive by his own wits, his strong work ethic, his ability to tough it out. Struggling once again with various business ventures, Robbie finally secured a low paying position with a merchandizing firm. Once again he rose to a supervisor position. Once again he asked his boss if it was possible for him to move up in the ranks and if he could earn $50,000 a year.

Once again he was told yes and yes. He had high hopes. He would move his family again to make this happen. He would fully commit his efforts. The final answer was the same as before. "Haven't heard back on your promotion," his supervisor said after a long two weeks.

Robbie was getting used to it. "Then I have to give my two weeks' notice to you," Robbie offered.

He finally realized that he couldn't rely on others. The government and companies and managers and other people had their own schedules, their own agendas.

He knew that if he truly wanted to succeed, if he really wanted to control his own life, if he absolutely wanted the best for his family, he would have to stick to his principles and run his own life.

And so he did.

The Perfect Pitch

Nine year old Toby Caine throws baseballs. He loves throwing the them. He loves baseball. Every day he throws one hundred pitches. Every day he works to be better. All he thinks about is baseball. After school. On weekends. All summer long. Even when he sleeps.

His father is a very impatient, mean, and demanding man. He torments his son for failing to throw strikes. He watches his boy throw the baseball. He shakes his head at each toss that's not a strike. He expects perfection and nothing else will do. He calls his son a loser. He denigrates the boy every day.

But Toby knows he's not a loser no matter what his father thinks or says. The boy is determined to throw only strikes. He keeps practicing. He ties an old tire hanging from a tree as his strike zone. It's at the perfect height for his age. Its open diameter is sixteen inches. An easy target. He steps back exactly forty-six feet from the tire. It's the perfect distance for his nine to twelve year old little league division.

His father continues to put his son down. He incessantly derides the boy. Toby hates his father, but he keeps practicing. Every day he carries a basket filled with one hundred old, scuffed-up baseballs. He pitches them into the tire opening. Most go through. Some bounce off. Others completely miss the target. He tries throwing left handed. It works just as well as right handed. He continues alternating his throwing arms. Three pitches with his right hand, then three pitches with his left hand. Same number of strikes and balls from both sides.

In time Toby sets up another makeshift, but smaller strike zone by replacing the large tire with a worn out wheelbarrow tire. The new target has an eight inch hole as the strike zone. He throws one hundred baseballs. Three lefty, then three righty. He throws an equal number of balls and strikes. Many go through the opening. Some bounce off. Others miss the smaller target completely.

Weeks later he changes to an even smaller circle, about as round as a small dolly tire. It's not much larger than the three inch diameter of a baseball itself. One hundred pitches. Three with his left arm, then again three with his right. Some go through the hole. Many bounce off. A few miss completely. But he doesn't give up. The boy is determined to be perfect. He is set on satisfying his father. He seeks approval from the man. But he mostly wants to prove to himself that he is good enough.

Toby plays in the town's Little League as a pitcher. He gets better as a strike-out pitcher, but still isn't perfect. He improves his fast ball pitch. Then his curve ball. Even later he develops his slider and sinker. Most of his pitches are strikes. Some don't come near the strike zone. Still, he is demeaned by his old man. But Toby doesn't quit. In private he continues to practice his pitching every day.

A few years later in high school he plays ball as a pitcher. He's not a spectacular pitcher, but he's good. Better than most other pitchers on his team. Better than most other pitchers in his age group. On occasion he pitches a complete game throwing more strikes than balls. Striking out more hitters than the other pitchers. The hatred for his father has built over the years. But so has the boy's need to be a perfect pitcher. He is determined to show his worthiness.

After graduating from high school Toby gets picked up as a pitcher for a minor league team. At first he doesn't get much playing time since he really is only a one-pitch thrower. Fast balls is his strong suit, but in the more competitive leagues a pitcher needs to be more diverse. After several months of passable pitching Toby moves up to an AAA team and waits for his opportunity to get into the big league. The Game. Where the real challenge is. Where true talent displays itself. Where he can prove what he is capable of. Where he can finally show his dad that he's not a loser, but a talented big league pitcher.

Fortune shines on the nineteen year old when two relief pitchers for the Boston Red Sox are injured in one game. He is called up to pitch at Fenway Park, should he be needed to fill a slot against the Yankees. The Red Sox are winning eight to five ahead of New York in their June outing. The manager pulls his struggling pitcher and calls for the new boy, Toby, to pitch in the eighth inning against three right-hand hitters. It's the heart of the Yankees line-up.

Toby readies himself in the bullpen. Minutes later he's on the mound and winds up to throw his first pitch in the big time. The catcher calls for a fast ball down the middle. Toby knows that pitch. It's his best. He throws a hard strike at ninety-nine miles per hour according to the backstop radar gun. The catcher nods his veteran approval toward the rookie pitcher. Toby feels comfortable despite the pressure situation he is in. He knows how to pitch. Damn it, he knows how to throw strikes.

His second pitch is another fastball strike which the hitter swings through. The young pitcher takes his time and winds up again. He throws his third strike ball directly into his tight strike zone. The hitter looks back at the catcher's glove as if to say, 'Where is it?' End of the inning. The catcher approaches Toby and pats him on his butt. "Great job kid!"

Toby feels good. He feels appreciated. Of course he is good pitching strikes. After all, that's what he does.

During the next series Toby remains in the pitching roster for quick one inning relief spots. He proves to be steady, reliable, though predictable in his fast ball throwing. Within a week the starting pitcher, fourth in the rotation, is put on the disabled list with a tender throwing elbow. Toby is penciled in by the team manager to pitch for the injured pitcher. He has confidence in the kid.

The second game in a series against the Nationals, the current last place team in the American League, is Toby's first game as a professional starting pitcher. Toby feels good. He feels confident. He pitches a fantastic first inning, striking out the side, throwing only nine pitches, all strikes over the plate or swung through. In the second inning he again throws only strikes, wheelbarrow tire strikes, strikes his father said he could never throw.

The game goes on. It's the top of the ninth inning. If Toby holds the opponent his team wins. Amazingly he's in line for a complete game. The first batter strikes out, swinging wildly at all three pitches. The second man up strikes out as well, violently swinging through empty air.

All 46,540 Boston fans are screaming their approval. "Toby! Toby! Toby!" The young pitcher hears the roar. The Red Sox are ahead one to zero. Toby sees the new batter called up to hit. T. Banner is one of the best pinch hitters in the league with a .384 batting average. With twenty-seven home runs for the season so far, and a well-known vengeance toward rookie pitchers, he steps up to the plate.

Toby sets and pitches. The umpire calls it a ball.

Toby waves at Rueb, his catcher, to talk. Most pitchers and catchers typically review their plan of attack and pitch selection for the massive home run hitter. The catcher puts his glove up to cover his mouth, just in case any member of the opposing team can read his lips and determine how the battery plans on pitching their power left-hand hitter.

"I don't need to pick the pitch," Toby says from behind his glove.

"Well, what's up?" the catcher asks.

Toby waves into the dugout. "I need my other glove," is all he says.

The manager, Rusty Malone, calls time and walks out to the mound along with the team doctor, Doc Moore, both men hoping Toby's pitching hand is alright.

"How you feeling son?" the manager asks.

"You okay?" the doc asks.

"I'm fine. Nothing's wrong," Toby answers. "It's just that with this hitter up I want my other glove."

The doc trots back to the dugout and tells the bat boy to get Toby's second glove from his tote bag. The boy obliges and retrieves the leather. He looks at it with a funny face but nonetheless runs out to the mound and hands it to Toby.

"Thanks Billy," Toby says, handing him his original glove.

Rusty the manager, Rueb the catcher, and all the infielders gathered at the pitcher's mound and look at the glove with confusion.

"What the hell's this?" Rusty says in a startled but not angry tone.

"I figured since the hitter is a lefty and with his record I need all the help I can get, so I'll throw left-handed," Toby answered as if it was no big deal.

"You never told us you could throw lefty... too," the manager said, still astonished by this discovery.

Toby looks down and kicks dirt from his cleats. "Up until now I never had to throw lefty. But with this guy," he nods toward the batter's box, "I need to use everything I've got."

The home plate umpire who had been unusually patient butts in to disperse the party to move the game along. "What's going on men?" he asks.

"My pitcher wants to switch to throwing left-handed," Rusty explains.

"He what?" the ump asks. "I never heard such a thing."

"Neither have I," the manager agrees.

"I'll have to check the rules book on that," the ump comments. He moves to the sideline and has the other umpires from first and second and third bases meet with him.

The National's manager comes out of the dugout toward the umpires. He wants to know what the holdup is. After learning of the situation he vehemently objects. "The pitcher can't do that! How can he switch his pitching in the middle of an at-bat? Who in the hell ever heard of a switch pitcher? What do the rules say?"

The umps check the rule book. Nothing mentions such a thing. Probably because it never happened before. They talk to both managers indicating that it apparently is allowed for a pitcher to switch pitching hands in the middle of a batter. Of course the opposing manager complains, but nothing is done about it. "There's no ruling against it. Let it go," the chief umpire says.

It wasn't until later in 2015 when official major league baseball rules addressed ambidextrous pitchers. The rule is actually referred to as the 'Pat Venditte Rule' which states that both pitchers and batters cannot switch hands in mid at-bats. But, pitchers are, according to the rules, allowed to switch their throwing arms against a new batter.

The Boston manager looks at his young pitcher Toby and nods. Rusty smiles at his rookie pitcher. "You've done great kid. This is your game. Get this guy out."

"Thanks skipper. I will," Toby says.

"Let's play ball men," the umpire yells out as he returns to his spot behind home plate.

The hitter, seeing Toby put his right-handed glove on, backs out of the batter's box and looks over at his manager with a what-the-hell-should-I-do look. His manager simply shrugs his shoulders in defeat. He moves his hands in a swinging motion as if to say, "Swing away."

The noise in the stadium revs up. All fans are on their feet for the last out. "Toby! Toby! Toby!" they shout.

Then there's a sudden silence. People start pointing at the pitcher. They can't believe their collective eyes. "He's

going to throw lefty." "How in the hell can he do that?"
"Did you know he could pitch both righty and lefty?" The
questions keep coming. Astonishment fills the entire
stadium.

The umpire yells, "Play ball" again. Even he couldn't
believe what he was about to observe. Inside he chuckles to
himself. 'Go for it kid,' he thinks. It was a long enough
delay. He points toward Toby. Time to finish this
astonishing ball game.

The hitter is a monster of a man. He stares a mean scowl
toward Toby. He mumbles something to his self. "You're
going down punk." He points his black bat at the pitcher's
throat. Intimidation is part of his game. He swings and
misses the first left-handed pitch. It whizzes past him at
ninety-four mph. Adjusting his stance he rips the second
fast ball toward the fence. It's high but curves just right of
the foul pole. A ninety-seven mph fast ball. Toby looks
around the stadium. It's so loud he can't hear the chatter
coming from his dug-out or his team members on the field.
His next pitch comes in at an astounding hundred and two
mph. It gets hit to a deep part of the ball park. To everyone
it looks like a game changing homer, but it veers off to the
left foul side line.

Toby focuses in on his catcher holding his mitt straight
out. One more strike and his team wins. In his mind Toby
sees the small circle strike zone, the one smaller than a
wheelbarrow opening. The four inch hole. He knows he can
do this. He isn't a loser. He never was a loser. Whatever his
father had called him before didn't matter.

He winds up and releases the baseball from his left
hand. His eyes follow the ball all the way to the plate. It
comes in at a snail's pace of only seventy-two mph. It slips
directly through the imaginary circle. The batter swings
wildly, missing the slow ball before it even hits the
catcher's mitt.

Game over. Toby wins.

It's a perfect outing for the rookie pitcher. A no-hitter. No base runners. Very few balls called. It's an unbelievable performance. But to Toby Caine it isn't a perfect game. To him a perfect game is all strikeouts. A perfect game is eighty-one pitches to twenty-seven batters, each pitch a strike.

And he continues to practice, because to him perfection is all that matters.

Saving America

They were not Americans.

The three men tossed their army green duffel bags into the trunk of their old, faded sedan, just as they had done many other times during their eight month stay. The car was a dark, four-door Chevy with stolen Texas plates provided by their local network of underground operatives.

All their needs had been arranged prior to them slipping into the country. It was much easier than they had anticipated, connecting with Miguel the Mexican smuggler in the small Sonoran town twenty miles south of the border. Miguel was a runner, a human smuggler, and a member of the large Latino gang known as MS-13, which Islamic infiltrators paid to penetrate the border. The mining town of Cananea was a staging point where guides, known in the business as coyotes, would lead their groups of paying, desperate humanity into the promised land.

But not all his customers were looking for work.

Five thousand U.S. dollars per head guaranteed the men would not be caught sneaking through the cut chain link fence a hundred yards west of the massive steel wall separating the two countries. From there they maintained a steady jog through the midnight shadows toward a waiting van less than a quarter of a mile from the fence perimeter.

Along with nearly one thousand immigrants attempting to make their way across the open border that night, the three Middle Easterners had disappeared into the moonless darkness. The dusty white van had been expertly lettered with U.S. Border Patrol green decals on its sides and counterfeit logos on its front doors. Just like the genuine ones. The driver, one of their countrymen, had his instructions to drive the terrorists straight through to South Phoenix, a three and a half-hour trip.

The rundown apartment they held up in was leased under a fictitious company heading. Utilities were turned on in the same false name. They even had cable television so they could watch how their associates scattered throughout the land were handling their special assignments. Results leading to disasters were always highlighted on the nightly news. American TV broadcasts were wonderfully informative.

If the stations only knew how helpful they were. Americans were so stupid. Under the impenetrable umbrella of their constitutionally protected free speech they told their enemies everything. The enemies within watched everything.

The men had been given fake passports with updated photos and new Arizona driver licenses that proved they had lived in the state for a number of years. Each of the men had also been issued untraceable cell phones that could easily be discarded or replaced if needed. Their every need was addressed. Money was never a problem. A taped envelope filled with enough cash for their expenses was stuffed into a locked mailbox at nine o'clock in the morning on the twenty-fifth of each month. All bills were paid in cash. All meals were eaten in the apartment. All communication went through their cell phones.

They were always ready to make their move.

Each of the insurgents carried a loaded sidearm tucked beneath his shirt. Should there be interference by anyone—a civilian, law enforcement, their landlord, the little old lady who walked her dog every morning past their place—they would not hesitate for one second to kill.

They were trained killers and followed their orders with a dedicated zeal. They knew the intricate diagrams of their targets. They identified the vulnerable spots of their intended objects and facilities to be destroyed. They studied the security systems they were about to breach. They knew the numerous code words better than their own fake names. They had all they could possibly need. Everything was in place for their one purpose in life.

The leader of the unit received a phone call directing them to be at their target in two hours. It was the same instructions they had gotten before, nineteen times before to be precise. None of the three men dared question whether this trip was another training exercise, a trial run, or the real thing. It wasn't their place to ask. It was only their duty to follow orders from an unseen chain of command. And there was absolutely no doubt they would follow instructions to perfection.

Even if it killed them.

Inside the car the oppressive August heat was barely cooled by the struggling air conditioner as the terrorists drove west along Interstate 10 through Phoenix in the late afternoon rush hour traffic. Blinded by the setting sun the driver was used to the heavy traffic, having traveled the same route toward their destination many times.

The Chevy stayed up with the flow of commuters, a mass of cars and trucks exceeding the speed limit by at least twenty miles per hour. If the other drivers only knew where the three where headed and what they intended to do, every citizen in his or her right mind would go home, pack up their family, and leave the city. But there really was no place for them to run. Every one of them would encounter the same disastrous end no matter where they turned.

Driving like an American the driver then turned eastbound on Buckeye Highway. They were headed toward the small town of Wintersburg secluded in the barren Arizona desert about fifty miles away. Every one of the four million citizens in the valley depended on the energy source from this hidden desolate territory. The heat waves hovering over the pavement reminded the terrorists of their homeland. But this was a different kind of desert heat. This was where their enemy lived. They missed not being home but their duty was here, in Satan's desert.

Their holy mission was similar to that of hundreds of other small terrorist cells lying low throughout the American landscape. They were all independent cells, though connected by larger, more powerful forces. Forces that very few people were aware of. Even the U.S. government. They were forces that could kill a superpower.

Stretched from coast to coast and border to border their comrades and associates, trainees and veterans, radicals and extremists, the entire network of terrorist organizations were preparing for their ultimate objective—to take over the United States of America.

Fearless and determined, they were committed to terrorize and annihilate. As faithful radical Islamic fundamentalists their God-given duty was to kill all non-believers—Christians, Jews, Westerners, Americans—all non-Muslims.

It was a long, bumpy, and dusty drive on the dirt road that turned off the highway. "Practice makes perfect," Ahmad said in clear English to the others, mimicking the old American saying.

Ahmad tightly held the steering wheel with both hands and was clearly the one in charge. "Perhaps today we will be allowed to show our allegiance toward Allah," he said.

He had been recruited by Hamas back home when his village was overrun by militant troops loyal to Islamic jihad. He was only twelve years old then, though it seemed much longer than ten years ago. He had become a dedicated soldier and felt honored to be chosen for this assignment.

Ahmad's brother, Yahya Hasan, a Jordanian who was much lighter skinned than his Syrian partners, sat quietly in the front passenger seat reviewing in his mind every step of their plan. Yahya, the youngest of the group at only sixteen, sat in the back and smiled. One day they would be honored as heroes, or even martyrs of their cause. It did not concern him whether he would live or die while completing his mission. It didn't matter to anyone of them. This was their destiny.

Each time they approached their target they meticulously checked their weapons, set their watches, timed their activities, studied the layout, planned their attack, prayed to Allah, envisioned the damage, monitored their GPS cell phones, and reviewed their alternate escape plans. Like devoted Islamic Muslims they were prepared to die for their cause but were more eager to kill as many infidels as possible.

As the sedan reached the sloping ridge the terrorists saw their familiar target. They parked the car under a clump of scrub mesquite trees and retrieved their satchels from the trunk. Carrying the heavy bags the men hiked their way along a footpath through scraggly cactus and over mounds of ancient slate rocks. At one of their four previously marked locations they began setting up their equipment.

From behind a pile of jagged slabs they looked down at their target nearly three thousand yards below them, knowing from experience they were safe from being seen. They focused on the monstrous structure spewing thick clouds of steam from the towering cooling chambers.

The Palo Verde nuclear power plant is a majestic example of modern engineering, though the facility had been built almost twenty years earlier. It's the largest nuclear plant in the entire country, with three active reactors on a four thousand acre site. The triple units together generate the largest capacity of electrical energy of all other sixty-five nuclear plants in the United States. Running at less than full capacity the power plant produces more than twenty-eight billion kilowatts of electricity providing power for millions of customers in the valley of the sun.

Americans were such wasteful energy hogs. A forced shut down of the complex would devastate the region, especially in the triple digit heat of the mid-summer. An attack on a nuclear plant would create havoc, confusion, and most importantly, nationwide terror.

Dressed in desert camouflage fatigues the militants methodically assembled the components of the Russian made rocket launcher and steadied its folding metal legs on a leveled patch of ground. One of the men made precise adjustments on a dial attached to the barrel of the weapon, slowly clicking one notch at a time while another terrorist looked through high-powered binoculars calling out coordinate numbers.

Six rocket rounds were placed on one of the flattened empty canvas bags, lined up and ready to be placed into the launcher. It took less than three minutes for the trio to get ready to commence their attack.

Islamic terrorists were well trained. Militant training camps were run in many Muslim countries throughout the Middle East. At the age of thirteen, young Muslim boys are conscripted as insurgents and spend between six and twelve months in various training camps located in one of the many Islamic friendly countries. At any given time at least thirty such camps were occupied, with upwards to five thousand recruits.

Soldiers of the cause were trained in use of weaponry, from simple hand-to-hand knife combat to the proper use of firearms—pistols, rapid fire automatics, and long range sniping rifles. They were taught how to operate high tech rocket mortars and cannons, and portable surface to arm missile launchers. A select group of insurgents were even trained to pilot small aircraft that could be used as flying weapons.

Trainees learned the ways of the West, in particular, the arrogant manners of Americans. They were also taught English so they could blend in as well as possible with crowds of multinationals in the larger cities and university students throughout the country. Though they had thick accents, their English was passable. They learned how to illegally enter through the porous borders along the southern boundaries, how to contact their sponsor groups waiting for their arrival, and how to become invisible and anonymous in plain sight.

They learned how to disrupt daily life at airports, on campuses, in cities, on the streets. They learned how to kill. Today they were ready. Soon the electric grid would be shut down and then all hell would break loose.

And no one could stop them.

Final Notice

Jack Baker was taking the long way as he drove home one afternoon. It was his birthday. Yesterday his wife had let it slip that their son and daughter, the grand kids, and a few friends would be coming over to the house tonight for cake and ice cream. Jack loved to see the kids. He especially loved seeing the little guys, his grandsons. They were great. So young and innocent and helpless with their entire lives ahead of them. Jack hoped they would have happy lives. He had just spent his last twenty-seven dollars on gifts for them.

The friends coming to the party were mostly his wife's friends. Sure, he knew them casually, but the truth was that Jack didn't have many friends. Not real friends. Not the kind a man could talk to. Not close enough friends to reveal what bothered him. Just people he knew.

Jack wasn't in much of a rush to celebrate his sixtieth birthday. In his own mindset there was very little to be happy about. The years had gone by too fast, like people always say. His life hadn't really turned out the way he wanted, the way he had planned. If he actually did plan it out.

Lots of his dreams and promises had gone by the wayside, discarded and forgotten in the rush of trying to make a living. Promises he had made to himself and to others. Especially those he had made to his wife Lanie.

It seemed there was never enough money or never enough time to do the things he wanted. Like take that once in a lifetime vacation. Lanie always dreamt of a trip to Paris. She was a good woman and deserved it. She deserved to have some fun in her life too. There was one time when they even got brochures on it. But it didn't happen. Or when they thought about buying a nicer house in a better neighborhood. Nothing extravagant, just something newer and safer for the kids. But that never happened. Or having enough money saved up for when he couldn't work or when it was time to retire. That was never going to happen either.

When he was a kid his dad always told him, "When you make a promise, you keep that promise. It doesn't matter who it was meant for, you keep that promise." But life and the years often prove that promises are sometimes hard to keep, maybe even impossible.

The old Ford pickup chugged along blowing blue smoke out the rear. He was riding down the same route he used to take from work, that is, when he had a job. Before the company was 'restructured' and 'cost reduction' efforts were put in place. Which meant hundreds of people, even those who had been employed at the same place for more than twenty years, including Jack, had been permanently laid off.

They were cut loose just like that, as if they were extra weight, useless to the company they had dedicated their working lives. Losing his job had taken something out of him, as if he had suddenly become worthless. As if he had no value left. That was a difficult challenge to a man who prided himself on his work. The unemployment checks were okay for a while, but they didn't last very long and had ended more than a year ago.

In an attempt to make ends meet Jack hired out to anyone who would pay him to do menial jobs like painting or yard work or minor household repairs. Sometimes it was pretty hard physical work, and at his age Jack tired easily. He was a good handyman and had most of the tools he needed to make a day's pay, when the infrequent work came in. But the pay was never enough to cover his bills. Not that he lived high on the hog or beyond his modest means. He had owned and lived in the same small three bedroom house for twenty-three years. It was the cutest little house on the block and had been meticulously maintained.

Jack was proud of his home, despite its age and short comings, and had enjoyed seeing his children grow up there. When they were much younger he and his wife Lanie would sit on the bench out front and watch their two kids ride their bicycles and play with their friends. In the summertime the ice cream truck showed up everyday day, its bell ringing and the kids licking their favorite treats. Those were good days, Jack remembered. He smiled a lot back then. He loved his wife more, enjoyed his children tremendously. He liked going to work. Jack Baker used to be a happy man.

It had been almost six months to the day since Jack and Lanie had lost their cute little home to the bank. The unemployment checks and Lanie's part-time income from working at the convenience store down the street weren't enough to save their house. The worst day in Jack's life was when he pulled into his driveway and saw an official looking poster taped to the outside of his front living room window. That's when he knew he was defeated.

The moment he caught glimpse of the notification he knew what it was. Exiting his truck he looked around at the neighboring houses hoping no one had seen the legal notice. How could this happen? He wondered. No, he knew how it happened, but he couldn't understand why. He had worked hard all his life. He did what he was told, was loyal to his company. In short, he had followed the rules like he was supposed to.

Jack had pursued the American dream. He went to school, got decent grades, served his country in the army, got married and had a nice family. He worked at a good firm, bought a house, paid his taxes. But apparently much of that didn't matter. Having an education didn't always help a man succeed if he didn't know the right people or didn't have the proper connections. Sacrificing for his country as a true patriot didn't necessarily earn what was promised. Working hard for his employer and remaining loyal to their needs didn't ensure longevity or a comfortable retirement. Not like before

He didn't know when everything went wrong. Things just crept up on him. Inch by inch life made its turns, its zigs and zags, some by his own doing and others not. Years tend to slip by without noticing how things change and then suddenly it hits you like a solid slap in the face.

He was constantly behind on his bills. The rent on the rundown house they were now renting. The electric bill that each month he scurried to pay before the power was shut off. He would often pay one bill and let another go late. The next month he would do the reverse. Sometimes he sold furniture from the house to pay the late bills. Money was always on his mind, always threatening him.

When Jack arrived home on his birthday he saw the mailman stuffing his box. There were always past due bills mixed with junk mail. Never checks. One letter stood out. It was certified and had to be signed for. Jack debated with himself whether to accept it or not. He had seen others like it before. Too many times. But this one had a large, bold, red-inked 'URGENT: FINAL NOTICE' stamped on the envelope. It was from the IRS. The Internal Revenue Service. An official statement from the U.S. government tac collector.

Two years earlier Jack had failed to file his taxes. He knew he owed money but he simply couldn't pay it. He foolishly thought if he merely let it go it would disappear. Vanish into thin air. He was a small fish in a giant pond. He would be overlooked and nothing would come of it. It was no excuse, purely a bad decision. And it had caught up to him.

The first letter he received from the IRS was merely a reminder. It was a straight form letter indicating that Mr.

Jack Baker had failed to file his tax forms for the previous two years. It said penalties and interest on the amounts due were accruing. It also instructed Jack to contact the regional revenue office to rectify the situation. Jack threw the letter away. Somehow he thought maybe the problem would simply go away.

At first he owed over seven-hundred dollars to the government in back taxes, interest, and penalties. Every couple of months he received another letter. Each new notice had higher fees with larger penalties added. Jack had always tossed the letters in the trash before Lanie could see them. Somehow he would take care of the situation. Somehow he would fix it.

He knew it was a mistake. He knew it was wrong. He knew it was taking a chance that he wouldn't get caught. But other obligations came first. Like the house payment and electric bill and clothes for his kids and food for his family. He intended to pay, when he could. But it seemed other things always happened first. His work truck needed tires, the washing machine broke down, doctor bills piled up. When he had the extra money, he assured himself, he would pay his taxes.

But the letters kept coming. Late fees and penalties and interest were going up each time. The last letter Jack had actually opened indicated that he then owed over twelve-hundred dollars. The notice was threatening, indicating serious steps would soon be taken to collect what was owed.

There were threats of garnishing his wages. But his side jobs were off the books and he was paid in cash. Because of that he paid his bills in cash or with money orders. There were warnings of taking his money from savings and checking accounts. But Jack had no savings accounts. His checking account was always at the minimum, just in case it got wiped out. There were menacing notices of possibly losing his property to the revenue service. But now he owned no property. He continued to hide the letters from his wife. He left the registered letter in his truck and went into his house.

He thought about the problem every day. Every time he checked the mail he worried that his life would be dramatically altered. Every time he saw the mailman drive by he worried. Every time he got paid from a small job he wanted to pay some to the government. But he knew it would never be enough.

Jack had nowhere to turn for help. By now he owed thousands of dollars to the IRS. He felt lost trying to live in the shadows. He had nothing of value to sell. No money. No prospects. No hope. At every turn he became more anxious. With every phone call he was afraid. Every knock at his door caused panic.

Lanie had his simple dinner ready. Pasta with sauce and bread and butter. Jack never complained. Dinner was always good. Lanie was a good cook. A good wife. A good partner. Jack knew he was a lucky man. He could see the sadness in her eyes. He knew of the losses she endured because her husband couldn't take care of her. Because he couldn't keep his promises. But she never said anything. She never mentioned it. She never put him down. She knew Jack was a good man in a bad place. She knew her husband was trying his best.

Jack ate his dinner, barely saying a word. He heard Lanie talking about the party but didn't pay much attention. He saw his birthday cake in a pink bakery box on the kitchen counter and wondered how much that had cost. He looked at the few cheap framed photographs Lanie had placed on the nearby bookcase. The two of them together in their earlier years when times were fun. When they had everything going for them. Pictures of their children playing and laughing and making a mess. Life had its moments.

After dinner Jack told his wife he had to go out for a few minutes. He wanted to pick up something for the grandkids, h lied. She reminded him to hurry up before everyone came for the party. He kissed her on the check and left.

Jack drove his truck away. He had no place in particular to go. He just had to drive. He had to think. He kept glancing at the IRS envelope, its large, bold, red-inked 'URGENT: FINAL NOTICE' screaming at him. He knew he had to open it, but he was afraid. He knew he had to read it if he had any chance to make things better. But he was terrified because he knew what was next. Everything they had would be taken away from them. He would be labeled a loser, a complete failure. He might even go to prison.

Jack Baker was a man at the end of his rope. He drove to a secluded area minutes from his house. He pulled off the road and stopped. The letter was on the seat beside him. He looked around. There was no one in sight. Jack picked up the envelope. He used his finger to tear open the top of the envelope. He stopped for a moment and turned off his truck. His life would change the second he read what would happen to him and his family.

He pulled the folded letter from the envelope and laid it back on the seat. He wasn't ready. All the mistakes and bad decisions and poor choices were piling up on him. He had let his family down. He had failed to keep his promises to his wife. And to himself. On the seat he touched the bag containing the grandkids' toys he had bought. He looked out the window and smiled. Then he began to cry.

Jack looked down the street. It was a hill with a sharp turn to the right at the end. He started his old truck again and put it in gear. He grabbed the steering wheel. Then he stepped on the gas. His foot pushed the pedal all the way to the floor. The truck picked up speed and raced down the hill. Jack took his hands off the wheel. He closed his eyes. In seconds it was over.

In the mangled wreckage at the bottom of the hill the letter on the seat flipped onto the passenger floor space. In his final seconds on this earth Jack never got to read the letter, which read:

"Dear taxpayer, after completing our investigation into your case it has been determined that tax levies, interest, penalties, and fees against you were erroneous due to an internal miscalculation. You are not liable for any past due taxes and no payments are currently due. Please disregard previous notices sent. We hope this hasn't been an inconvenience to you. Have a nice day."

Of Sons and Daughters

My dad was a good man. As a young boy, like most sons, I wanted to grow up to be like my father. Unfortunately, that's exactly what happened.

I woke up just before midnight to familiar sounds coming from the kitchen. The noise sounded like soft, muffled sniffles, like when I had a cold last winter and didn't bother to wipe my nose. I've heard the same sounds before, too many times late in the night, and it scared the hell out of me.

A dim yellow light seeped around my partly closed bedroom door off the narrow hall. I quietly snuck out of my bed, hoping not to wake up my younger brothers in their bunk beds just four feet on the other side of our room. I slowly opened my door enough to peek around the corner into the kitchen. At only nine years old the noise had already changed my entire outlook on life and had stayed with me over these past sixty years.

My father was sitting at the small table in our tiny kitchen. He often did that after mom and we boys went to bed. His broad back was facing me and he was still wearing his factory work uniform, even this late into the night. I heard him sniffle again, deeper this time, and it made me feel sad. He was looking down at something. I couldn't see in front of him. Without seeing his face, though, I could tell something was wrong and it worried me.

Was he sick? No. Dad never got sick, I thought. Never. He went to work every day early in the morning, before Eddie and Steve and I went to school during the school year, or like now, when we slept in on our summer vacation. Every night he came home at the same time, six o'clock, as mom was preparing our supper. At meal time we sat at the table while dad talked to us and mom about the same things every day. He was a good man and a good father, but there was always a sense of anxiety in his look.

That night I could see my father wiping his eyes with his hand as he concentrated on the ever-present notepad. Dad always had something to write on when he sat at the kitchen table. He always doodled or played with numbers or drew out intricate designs. His little book, scraps of paper or matchbook covers or folded napkins were his writing materials. I once asked him what he was doing as he scribbled on his pad. "Just thinking," he calmly said with a forced smile. "Just thinking about things," he answered.

My dad was a very smart man. Smarter than any other man I knew, even though he had never finished school. Smarter than my uncles and his friends and our neighbors. He knew everything. He knew about his work and the city and history and geography and money. And he knew numbers. He could add up a long list of numbers without writing them down. In his head he could figure fractions and percentages faster than my math teacher. When I grow up, I used to think to myself, I wanted to be as smart as my dad. I so much wanted to be like him.

I silently watched my troubled father as he took a sip of tea. That's what he drank at night. In the morning too. I could see two used tea bags lying on the side of his saucer. Since I was certain my father wasn't ill. I figured he was worried over money. On other occasions, after Dad had left for work, I looked through his notepad. It was filled with numbers and dollar signs crossed out or scribbled over. I was certain he was a genius. Some numbers had circles gouged around them.

I remember one day Dad and Uncle Ronnie were on the screened-in front porch of our tiny country cottage talking about their work and money. Grown up stuff. "I'll never work for less than a dollar an hour," my father said. He was a proud man willing to do whatever he had to for his family, but he had principles.

"You can't support a growing family on a buck an hour," my uncle argued as they continued their griping about work and money. "We're better than that," he continued. "You know we're worth more than a dollar an hour."

A dollar an hour sounded pretty good to me. I was good with math too and quickly calculated a man working forty hours a week would earn just over two thousand dollars a year. Wow! That was a fortune, I thought.

I got a dime allowance every Saturday, but only if I took out the trash every day, made my bed, and helped my brothers pick up our room. Ten cents a week could buy me a handful of penny candy from the corner store down near the lake. I could buy used comic books from my friends for only a nickel each. If I spent all my money in one week I was out of luck until the next weekend rolled around. So I supplemented my income by finding soda bottles tossed along the road leading to the town beach. The extra two cents for each recovered bottle supplied me with ice cream cones and maybe a Coke of my own.

That was my full extend of the knowledge of money. A kid my age could get by with very little. A father, I guessed, with a house and a car, a wife, and three growing boys, needed a lot more. He probably needed even more than two thousand dollars a year. I felt bad for my father and wished he could make more money. Maybe I could find extra soda bottles in the woods to help him or skip my allowance. But that would never be enough.

As I grew up I began to fully realize the financial difficulties my father and mother had struggled with. Dad worked every day and finally reached the buck an hour pay which I guessed was the going rate for unskilled workers in the late 1950s. Mom cleaned and cooked and took care of her sons. As my brothers and I grew, our house got smaller and our clothes got older. And Dad looked more tired and beaten. He continued trying his best but I knew inside it was never enough. The midnight sessions of drinking tea and doodling were constant reminders of things not meant to be.

When I turned sixteen and was halfway through high school I got a part-time job at the local grocery store. I helped a little with the food bills but was mostly concerned with getting me a car and having fun with my friends. Teenagers tend to be self-centered and don't think much about their families. They distance themselves from them.

One day after walking home from school I saw an ambulance way down the road parked on the dirt driveway in front of our house. I dropped my books and ran to the front porch. Without anyone saying anything I knew what had happened. Mom was crying as the medics rolled out a gurney toward the rear of the ambulance. Dad was in bad shape. Fortunately, that time he recovered from his second heart attack, but never completely. Life's struggles had crushed and defeated him.

At one time it occurred to me that I hadn't spoken to him in weeks. I hadn't said anything nice to him in a long time. I hadn't ever said "I love you Dad." Never. I mean, never in my whole life did I say those words. I was afraid my life would mirror his. I was afraid I would grow up to be just like him.

I know things about my dad that no one else still alive knows. I remember when my younger brother Steve was sick many years ago. Dad and Mom stayed with him at the hospital, day and night, for more than two weeks, even though Dad needed to work.

I remember asking for a new bike when I was seven, never really expecting such an expensive gift. On Christmas Eve when my brothers and I were woken to open our few presents, there was a brand new shiny blue bike beside the tree.

I remember when I went into the Air Force, Mom told me Dad had cried after his oldest son was gone, never knowing when I would return. And again when his other son, Eddie, had gone off to war. It was not until that time I realized how much my father really loved his boys.

Dad was a good father, though most of his waking moments were him working to give his family as comfortable a life as possible. As a teenager, like most, I was rebellious and somewhat aloof from my parents. There was no malice intended, but that's how growing kids react. Later in my life I regretted my behavior and wanted to make amends before it was too late.

After the military, as a young immature man with a growing family of my own, I learned how a father truly cares for and loves his children. I saw things I had admired in my dad and tried my best to emulate them. I saw the love in my mother's heart and wanted to be like her as well. My wife Pen and I had a handsome, intelligent, outgoing, curious, friendly little boy, Larry. He was the joy of our lives. From the day he was born in Bangkok, Thailand, to this very day decades later, he has brought happiness to us. It was up to me to help Larry become a great human being. But it was mostly his mother who did that.

Our beautiful curly haired baby daughter Melinda filled our lives. She was a godsend to us. I would never have imagined the wonderful things that could be learned from such a happy and loving child. But, unfortunately, there were many times I didn't listen, I didn't see the wonderful miracles right in front of me. I was spending most of my time working. I was trying to get ahead. I was more focused on making money than making memories with my family. I had fallen into the trap and didn't know how to get out of it.

I made one major mistake in my life which I regret even to this day. It was a bittersweet decision. One that most every man makes without realizing the consequences of his actions, although well intended. Everything a person does puts something in motion. It redirects, causes different reactions, different results. Everything one does changes his future in one way or another. Good, bad, or neutral. And most often it's not felt until after it's done.

We were a young couple with young children. I had the same attitude as my dad concerning working for others and earning what I thought I was worth. I had made a unilateral decision to pack up, move away from the old homestead and try to make my fortune in life. We sold our small home, loaded up a trailer, and headed west in search of wealth, independence, and our destiny.

In our wake we had left behind things we never thought we would miss. Things we could never recapture. We left behind people we had somehow forgotten were most important to us. Mom and Dad remained strong. They smiled and waved goodbye as we left them for the unknown thousands of miles away. They wished us luck and good fortune. They insisted we call them at least every week. They loved us more than I ever knew. They promised that someday they would visit us.

Without looking back we drove away from all we had known, with hope and promise in our hearts. In the rearview mirror I could see my father wiping his eyes as his son and daughter-in-law and two beautiful grandkids went down the road. It was at that very instant when I realized how much he would miss us, but mostly the kids. I realized how much our move had hurt him and my mom. But I kept driving toward our new life, unable to speak for many miles ahead.

I think of that day many times now as our grown children have ventured out on their own, gone their own way, and took risks in search of their futures. Like my dad I missed my children when they moved away or were too busy or made mistakes. And again, like my dad, I missed my grandchildren with whom I so wanted to be an integral part of their lives.

But life goes on, as they say. People grow. And in the end, it's a good thing.

Under All Is Land

Under all is land. That's the simple and accurate axiom in the preamble of the real estate bible. Just look under your feet. Good old terra firma. It's everywhere. Land is the fundamental basis of all real estate.

I'm sure you've heard the saying, "Location, Location, Location" when dealing in real estate. That just about sums up the intrinsic value of property anywhere in the world. The most important element in real estate is WHERE. Ocean front, good; swamp land, bad. Well, maybe. Then there's the WHEN. Timing is very important too. Economic recession, bad; hot market, good. Possibly.

When you decide to invest in real estate, whether it's in your first modest little house, a more expansive move up home, a vacation getaway, a rental income property, land speculation, or for you really aggressive investors who concentrate on apartment complexes, commercial properties, or even subdivisions, TIMING and LOCATION are crucial factors.

Now I'm not going to bore you guys to death with a wheelbarrow load of details surrounding mortgage options, property selections, contract strategies, and a ton of other details in the real estate world. Hey, that stuff is a must know, but there are thousands of formats out there which offer the finer points necessary for you to make a prudent decision in the world of real estate investing.

I'm sure you've probably read dozens of books yourself looking for the elusive silver bullet to riches. I'm certain you've also watched a bunch of slick videos or attended numerous 'free' seminars in search of those 'secret' pieces of advice leading you toward your real estate goals. They all promise you can become a multi-millionaire overnight, become financially independent working only a few hours a month, live the life you and your family deserve, drink champagne and watch soap operas all day while your envious neighbors trudge off to work and give you suspicious looks as they head out the driveway to their miserable jobs. And it all comes with a 100% money back guarantee.

How's all that stuff you've read and heard working for you? Well, don't believe most of it. Investing in real estate is hard work. It's a risky business packed with unforeseen pitfalls which can be emotionally exhausting and financially demanding. It can make or break you if you don't have a strong conviction, or an unwavering commitment, and guts of steel. Having some cash or good credit will come in handy too. And you can never discount the moral support from your spouse, family, and friends. Believe me, you're gonna need it.

You won't find all that hype or trivia in these pages, though on occasion we might peer into the tool box of basic real estate nuts and bolts. We may even trip over a few nuggets of pure genius, a pot load of luck, and some very unconventional transactions. Let's not kid ourselves. Real estate investing is often difficult. It's typically stressful, sometimes unpredictable, and generally a pain in the butt. There will be occasions when you'll wonder why in the hell you ever got into such a mess. There will be times when you'll lose, not only your cool, but on occasions your money. You'll freak out, have sleepless nights, wonder why in the hell nobody else ever does what they're hired to do, develop episodes of unabashed cursing that would blush a seasoned sailor, and in general simply curse the day you ever became an investor.

However, it can be enjoyable and quite profitable. It can even be fun and spiritually refreshing. In this gig you benefit from what you put into it. And one thing is for certain, it beats working for 'the man.'

The real point here is not so much to lecture on how to invest in real estate, but instead to help stimulate and hopefully inspire you enough to get off the damn couch and do something about it. You really have to want to do this, otherwise just keep going to your day job like the rest of the slugs and quit complaining about your 'situation.'

You've heard the stories about the oddball down the street who bought a few rentals and became filthy rich, or about the kid fresh out of school who bought a chunk of land on credit and retired before his thirtieth birthday. It can be done. This venture can change your life. It really can. Or maybe it can fulfill some of those cloudy dreams you have of living a little bit better than you are now. But only you can decide. Only you can motivate yourself to learn and get out there and do it. Frankly, in the real world, nobody else really cares if you succeed or not, so it is totally up to you my friend. And let's face it. If that guy down the street can do it, why can't you?

Getting rich in real estate ain't all that easy, but it can be done. So let's go through the important things you must know when investing in real property and look at a handful of examples that have gotten me to where I am today. But before we travel that road I should introduce myself along with my humble accomplishments, my miserable failures, and my deeply embedded passion to play the real estate game. I am by no means a real estate mogul like Donald

Trump. I'm a regular guy who has worked it and for whom real estate has been "very, very good to me."

Just so you know that I've paid my dues investing in real estate and have, through sheer longevity and effort, and I must admit, osmosis, figured out a few things you need to do in order to succeed in this business.

I've been investing in real estate in one form or another since 1975, when I was young and stupid. Now I'm older and not as stupid. Over the decades I have personally bought and sold eighty properties, and still counting...if my wife lets me. I was a very active and productive real estate agent for twenty years. During the majority of that time I was co-owner, manager, trainer, and front-line janitor of a successful real estate firm in southern Arizona during which time I represented more than a thousand home buyers and sellers in their transactions.

I have owned numerous rental properties, flipped dozens of fixer-upper houses, developed land-home packages, represented home builders, did land splits, sold commercial properties, and carried residential notes. I've also lost properties to foreclosure, chased low-life tenants after they made their midnight moves, fell behind on payments, and got stuck in a downward market. Hey, that's real estate.

In my opinion education is foremost and I had earned numerous higher level designations in the real estate field as a Realtor and was always learning new things in the industry. In other words I've been around the block a few times and have actually hit my target more often than not. So, have fun my friends. Hope you learn a few tips that help you buy and sell properties and make some money.

Here's a disclaimer. I won't pretend to know it all by giving you legal, accounting, or tax advice, which I am not. I do, however, recommend that you seek counsel from a real estate attorney, guidance from a competent accountant, and direction from a knowledgeable tax person. All three of mine should be paroled within the next few years, except for my accountant, of course, who apparently got a little too creative with his own books and will be working for our government gratis for some time to come. You may also want to put a professional shrink on retainer. Just in case.

Man Laws

NOTE: To those who are easily offended by words they don't like, behavior they disagree with, and generalizations they oppose, these man laws are listed as a fun, sarcastic, and tongue-in-cheek look at the human male species' conduct and weird mindset. If you feel slighted by these assertions then it may be time for you to go hug your teddy bear.

1. Once divorced, never marry again, rent it.
2. Have a secret cash account hidden somewhere.
3. Real men do not wear fanny packs.
4. Men take care of the family finances.
5. Real men do not drink foo-foo drinks.
6. Men don't discuss their work at home.
7. Lesbianism is OK.
8. Men never look over when the next urinal is being used.
9. Men have to look at women's cleavage.
10. Men wash their woman's car.
11. Real men only eat salad *at* home.
12. Real men don't cry, unless their team losses.
13. Beer is a breakfast food.
14. The BBQ grill belongs to the man.
15. Men don't drive scooters.
16. No matter how gorgeous she is, there's some guy out there who is sick and tired of taking her shit.
17. All men fantasize.
18. Size always matters.
19. Women should not be sports announcers.

20. Never buy a woman a nail gun.
21. When your wife is pissed off, sleep on your stomach.
22. When a woman calls you by your proper name, you are in trouble.
23. Never mention your secretary's name at home.
24. Men need their own room, woman have the kitchen.
25. Real men don't shop.
26. The TV remote belongs to the man.
27. Men are allowed power naps.
28. Your wife's girlfriends are off limits.
29. Have a private e-mail account.
30. Beer is a health food.
31. Feminine hygiene items belong in a separate medicine cabinet.
32. Old girlfriends cannot be your friends.
33. Real men do not drink wine coolies.
34. T-shirts cannot be worn for more than three days straight.
35. Only two days for socks.
36. The garage belongs to the man.
37. Women should never clean up the workshop.
38. Real men never ask for directions.
39. Women know everything.
40. Keep your pants on while driving.
41. Whenever you rent a hotel room, you must get laid.
42. Viagra is good.
43. Men must worship women's thongs.
44. Real men carry their money next to their boys.
45. ATM and debit cards are for wimps.
46. Don't ever go home smelling of perfume.
47. Near beer is for pussies.
48. Don't ever ask how her day was.
49. Never tell her she's fat.
50. Look at her mother first.
51. Never say I love you during sex. Or thank you.

52. Stay out of the kitchen.
53. Sign your own paycheck.
54. The man always drives.
55. Seeing a woman walk down the street, a man has only a fraction of a second to decide—yes or no.
56. Don't judge the face by looking at her long hair from the back.
57. Whiskers on a woman should be a red flag.
58. Check her teeth before marrying her.
59. Women should leave the toilet seat up.
60. Don't ever act happy to work late.
61. Never talk in your sleep.
62. Never smile in your sleep.
63. Never laugh in your sleep.
64. Don't ever tell her how much you lost—or won—on a bet.
65. Beer bottles are not flower vases.
66. Anything with wheels and tits will cause you trouble.
67. Don't tell your wife about your retirement.
68. On birthdays, Valentine's Day, anniversaries, and Christmas, do not believe it when she says, "Oh, you don't have to get me anything."
69. Men hide their cell phone pictures.
70. "Yes dear," is the only acceptable answer.

Saving Sara

Jamie was playing in the park next to his house. Like most five year old boys he liked hanging on the jungle gym and soaring on the swings. Every afternoon after preschool, Jamie and his mother and his twin sister Sara would go to the park. His mother would pack a small picnic lunch for the three of them. PB & J sandwiches, crackers and cheese slices, grapes or raisins, and cookies she had baked.

Jamie usually ran off on his own toward the swing sets as his mother watched. He was a typical energetic little boy who needed to burn off his excess energy. He would get dirty from playing and sweaty from running and scraped from falling. But he would keep going until his mother called for them to go into the house to clean up and hopefully take a short afternoon nap.

Sara, on the other hand, was different. She would tire easily. She was afraid of the swings and stayed close to her mother. She didn't much care for spending time in the park. Their private picnics were fun, but she preferred staying indoors where it was safe and cool and clean.

One morning Jamie took the small school bus in front of his house to his half-day preschool session. He liked school. He had lots of friends his age there. The school also had a playground with swings and see-saws and slides. Every recess that was where Jamie played.

That particular day his sister was ill and stayed home from school with her mom. By mid-morning the little girl told her mother she was feeling much better. Her temperature had gone down. Mom decided it would be good to take Sara outside and sit in the sun. The warmth and fresh air would do her good. Some younger children were on the swings and Sara boldly went to see them.

And then it happened.

Mom called to her daughter to stay away from the moving swings. Sara turned to her mother just as one of the swinging seats slammed into the back of her head. She fell to the ground without a sound. The kids pushing the swings ran to their mothers on benches nearby. They were crying at what they had done.

Sara didn't move. She was faced down in the grass. A large gash in her skull was bleeding heavily. Her curly blond hair was matted with dirt and blood. Mom ran to her baby, screaming. The other mothers ran to the fallen child. One of them called 911 on her cell phone. Sara's mother cradled her injured little girl in her arms. Blood continued to flow from the girl's head.

Within five minutes an ambulance had arrived. The paramedics checked the girl's vital signs, put a temporary bandage on the child's wound, and lifted her off in a gurney. Her mother, of course, went with her. In the ambulance she called her husband at work. She told him what had happened. She told him they would be at the hospital. She also told him to pick up Jamie at his school.

The doctors did their best to stabilize Sara, but she had lost a lot of blood. Tests were quickly run. Tubes were inserted into her arms. She was hooked up to an array of monitoring machines. The doctors were doing everything they could to save Sara.

Her mother was frantically pacing in the waiting room praying. Her husband had arrived with their son Jamie. Worry was on their faces. Jamie cried for his sister. He really didn't understand the situation. He just knew that his younger twin sister—by eight minutes—was in trouble.

Blood tests showed that Sara had O-Negative type blood. O-Negative blood is one of the rarest types. It can be transfused into most patients with other types of blood, but O-Negative patients can only receive O-Negative blood. Unfortunately, there are times when hospitals and blood banks have no O-Negative blood available. This was one of those times and time was urgent.

The doctors got blood samples from Sara's parents. Blood was needed now. Both parents had AB type blood which could not be transfused into their daughter. Hope was slipping away as the little girl languished in the hospital bed. Then one of the doctors saw the son, Jamie. They asked for and got a blood sample from the boy which turned out to be O-Negative, a perfect match for the girl.

Jamie heard the doctor talking to his parents. "It's a matter of life and death," he had told them. They agreed that Jamie's blood could save their daughter.

"Jamie," his mother said to him in the quiet waiting room. "You and Sara have the same kind of blood. You can save her. Would it be okay if the doctor took some of your blood and gave it to Sara?"

His mother was crying. Jamie could see how important this was. Jamie loved his sister. He was always supposed to watch out for her. It was his job to protect her. He would do anything for his baby sister.

Jaime was silent for a few seconds. He knew what had to be done. He looked at his mother, than his father, and finally the doctor. He was a strong kid. "I can do that," he said.

His mother hugged him. The doctor shook his hand. "You're a brave young man," he said.

The transfusion went well, as expected. Young Sara's condition improved. She would fully recover, although the doctor said she would have to remain in the hospital for several more days under precautionary observation.

Jamie and his Mom and his Dad restlessly sat in the lounge. The doctor arrived and shared the good news. He stooped down to Jamie and said, "You are a very courageous boy. You saved your sister's life."

Jamie looked at the doctor. Tears were in his eyes. He was afraid.

"What's wrong, son?" his Dad asked.

Jamie wiped the tears from his cheeks and asked, "So when do I die?"

"Oh, Jamie," his father said. "Why do you say that?"

The little boy was afraid. "Because I gave my blood to Sara."

"You're going to be fine, Jamie," his mother reassured him. She pulled her unselfish son to her chest. She turned to her husband and they all began to cry.

Young Jamie believed, as a five year old might, that by donating his blood to save his sick sister Sara he would have to give up his own life. And he had done it without question.

The Reckoning

Leaving the site of the concentration camp massacre, Cody Gordon was driving his rescued family back to safety. The week-long arctic vortex had let up a bit allowing an early snowfall to begin. In the November deep freeze the heat from the Humvee's vents felt good. It would take most of the afternoon and into the night for him to retrace his tracks through the barren, death-ridden landscape into the haven of the small compound seated in the back shadows of the Huachuca Mountains.

With a tense smile Cody glanced over at his wife in the passenger seat, and through the rear mirror viewed the sleeping children packed in the back. He knew this escape was their only hope. In a moment still strange to him he prayed he could save them. He prayed he could shelter them from the newly released evils they had barely survived. He also silently prayed they would not encounter trouble along the way.

His wife Robin, bundled in a green army blanket, rocked side to side as she rested half asleep while the solid vehicle slowly rambled threw the rocky desert terrain. During the past few days Robin had seen things no one in America could ever think they would witness. She had survived with their children the vicious kidnapping from their home and endured the vile camp conditions. She had lived through the slaughter of innocent victims, the brutality of the soldiers bearing down their automatic weapons and tower machine guns on those imprisoned. She had seen death at every step of her incredible ordeal.

Thick thorny bushes and low hanging mesquite branches scraped the sides of the truck as Cody maneuvered through the dry washes of the reservation. Following the trail to the highway would be easy. One way in, one way out. The difficult part would be locating the obscure turn-offs hidden in the mountain forest as he neared his destination closer to the international border.

The Gordon's young children, Jennifer and Jeffrey, were snug in their sleeping bags passed out after their horrendous experience in the death camp. Thank God their mother was strong, Cody thought. He feared what they had lived through would stay with them for the rest of their lives. They were just little kids and they were scared beyond belief. No one should be put through such terror, he thought, least of all young, innocent children.

What they had just survived would most certainly alter their world view as they grew older, if they ever had the chance.

Cody was afraid too. Nothing in his forty-two years had ever prepared him for what had happened. He was unsure what he should do. Nothing had been certain over the past few days. But everyone in the vehicle depended on him for their survival. There was no way in hell he was going to fail them now.

Two other little passengers slept warm and comfortable in the back seat. They were also wrapped in their protective sleeping bags. Traumatized by recent events, the neighbor girls Caitlin and Tanya were now the responsibility of Cody and Robin. Their parents Nick and Lisa had been murdered in the bloody camp mayhem, collateral loses in the all-out war on American soil against every American citizen.

Life was about to drastically change for them all.

Cody felt overwhelmed. Things had changed so suddenly, so severely. Just a few days ago he had returned home from his teaching position at the local college to enjoy the long Thanksgiving weekend with his family. He was just a history teacher, a simple family man who never caused, nor looked for trouble. He didn't like confrontation. He learned to get along even when he saw things go wrong.

But what could he do?

He was nobody.

Just a guy.

A father doing his best to care for his family.

On that day in the kitchen Robin had been getting some things ready for their holiday dinner. Preparing the turkey for an all-night slow roast. Making the stuffing and the traditional trimmings. Defrosting the pumpkin and apple pies. The kids were watching The *Wizard of Oz* in their pajamas in front of the warm fireplace. The unusually cold weather had shut down the city. Streets were empty, stores were closed, and most everyone had hunkered down for a casual, relaxing evening in their homes.

Then the lights went out.

And the furnaces shut down.

And the water stopped running.

And the phones went dead.

Land lines and cells.

And the radios didn't work.

Even with batteries.

And the Internet crashed.

And vehicles wouldn't start.

And panic set in.

And the night grew colder.

Much colder.

The bad things began to happen.

And people turned for help.

But there was no help.

And then they began to die.

His family had been taken and transported to the camp in the middle of the desert on the Pascua Indian Reservation south of Tucson. Most every family in the small city where they lived was removed as well. To a safer place, they were told. To warmth where food and medical attention were awaiting them, they were assured. To temporary refuge where they could stay until the terrible storm resided, they were promised. A sanctuary where the cold and scared citizens of the city could wait in safety and comfort while the electricity and heat and water were restored in their homes.

Lies.

All lies.

But those who complained were forcefully extracted by the soldiers of fortune. Those who refused to leave their homes were instantly shot in their living rooms by foreign troops canvassing the neighborhoods. Those who were stranded far from their homes were left to die in the frigid cold. But most of the people followed the bizarre orders like sheep being herded to slaughter. False promises of food and water and heat and security far outweighed the natural instincts of the people to question the move.

So they boarded the buses and let the soldiers push them and followed the rules and hoped for the best. They groaned and wept, they screamed and cried. But they did as they were told despite ingrained suspicions and unorthodox procedures. Old men and younger males, grandmothers and middle aged women, teenagers and very young children.

They all filed into the transports as directed, waiting for this horrible night to be over with.

But in truth, it had just begun.

All firearms and weapons had been confiscated by the unusual soldiers. Small arms for personal protection and hunting rifles for leisurely sport were appropriated for the safety of the people.

An unarmed populace was easier to control.

Easier to manage.

And far easier to eliminate.

Later, after the masses were relocated, all forms of personal wealth were routinely removed from their vacant houses without anyone's notice or question. The owners would have no further need for their valued possessions.

And that was only the beginning.

People died in their stalled cars, on the city streets, on the still highways. Most simply froze to death from the near zero degree temperatures. Others attempted to get to their homes on foot after their vehicles had inexplicably stalled. But few would survive the vicious freeze. Roving gangs of miscreants hit the streets in their primal search for easy pickings as the common civilized world quickly evolved back into its primitive stage.

Small groups of brave or desperate citizens, typically traveling in twos and threes, left their houses looking for answers from the authorities. Where were the police? Where were the forces promising to serve and to protect? But there was no help. There were no answers, no assurances, no semblance of orderly safeguard. People were left to rely solely of their own defenses.

And for most that meant the end was near.

Cody steered the Humvee off the dirt path onto the highway going north away from the Mexican border. There were no cars running on the darken road. No lights ahead or behind for miles in either direction. Despite the accumulating snow on the slick pavement he raced the vehicle as quickly as it would go. He drove past hundreds of disabled vehicles on the road. He swerved around the abandoned or crashed cars and trucks. Snow-covered frozen lumps lying in the street and on the side shoulders revealed the unlucky souls who failed to find their way home.

He was worried, scared, anxious.

But not like before.

Not like when this all began to happen. Cody's mind was alert, peaked. Built up adrenaline had driven him. His injuries from the morning's battle ached beyond belief. But he refused to accept the throbbing pains in his side and leg.

He had to do this one thing right. He had to get his family to the safe place.

The cab of the vehicle was quiet and he was glad of it. He felt the urge growing inside him. Deep in the unknown and untouched soul of a man. Someplace where a person's essence lives.

He sensed the changes within.

Purpose taking hold.

Intervention directing him.

Determination guiding him.

He envisioned the written note that old man Jack had passed on to him when he died, when this unholy hell had started. He couldn't get it out of his mind. The words were embedded in him like a tattoo in relief, as if they were struck in stone. They seemed a prophetic scar of moral duty.

Simple.

Pointed.

True.

Meant for him.

It read. *"Bad things happen when good men do nothing."*

Cody knew what he was destined to do next.

First chapter of author's sequel book,
Treasonous Behavior, The Reckoning

Never Too Late

Brandon had decided. He knew what he wanted. He always knew what he wanted. It was finally time to move forward to where he really belonged. "When you change the way you look at things, the things you look at change," he remembered the bold, inspirational saying. It was so true.

He told his friends and family that he had to go on a trip and might be gone for some time. Might never come back. No questions were asked. No explanation needed. He said so long to his longtime friend and business partner. Taylor knew where he was headed. His kids wished him well. They probably knew too. It was definitely time to enjoy the rest of his life. Loneliness was not a good partner.

Carpe diem and all that. Seize the day.

The man knew exactly where he was going. He had considered the move for quite some time. Ever since his wife had…well, he'd leave it at that. Brandon took a plane, then a long uncomfortable bus ride, and then a taxi to where he hoped he would be happy once again. Things can get crazy sometimes. This was one of those crazy times. Live life to the fullest. He remembered the prophetic words.

It was years ago but he still remembered the wonderful moments he had let slip pass. He remembered their coffee times, going away to enjoy each other's company. Their silly jokes and constant e-mails. Their marathon conversations and their simple gifts of sincere friendship brought a smile to his aging face. God, he even loved the way she ate her morning toast.

He still carried the silver blessing coin she had given him so many years ago when they were about to call it quits. At this very moment he was rubbing it like a worry stone, feeling its worn edges between his clenched fingers.

He made a point of having it with him every single day. It was most certainly his good luck piece.

He remembered how in a surprisingly short period of time he accidentally became attached to this wonderfully uninhibited lady as he learned more about her and slowly began to unveil her inner beauty. She was indeed a gorgeous woman, but more importantly she was a terrifically beautiful person. 'Refreshing' was the word that came to mind whenever he thought of her.

Brandon especially remembered her sweet child-like giggling, her kindness, and abundant thoughtfulness. And every day he remembered how eventually, without planning, without any purposeful intention, he had simply fallen in love with her. Sometimes love just happens, he thought. She had absolutely captivated him. His falling for her most certainly was not deliberate, but what he was doing now sure was.

Riding in the back seat of the bumpy taxi Brandon couldn't stop smiling as he recalled their songs. The driver kept looking in the rear view mirror thinking he had an idiot gringo passenger singing to himself. There was *Unchained Melody* accompanied by a too brief and very restrained slow dance that cold morning long ago. Willy's *You Were Always On My Mind*, was always on his mind.

He remembered how she was afraid to say the words "I love you" because of their situations. At the time it was perhaps the right thing to do (or not to do). But, what if? He wondered. What if they had simply let go back then?

In particular he remembered when at one point he risked everything and told her that he would marry her "if things were different" and how she had accepted his proposal "most definitely," if things were different too. Life was complicated for both of them back then.

Well, things were different now.

He also remembered when she was hurt with the bittersweet 'it's over' e-mail. He could still hear her quivering voice telling him over the phone, "I miss you already," before he even left her. It hurt him too.

Life was fun with her. That was a certainty. After these many years he still remembered all that. He remembered everything, in fact. The wonderful secrets and dreams and desires they so briefly shared. They had 'it.' He wanted it all back again. Now! It wasn't too late, he convinced himself.

The dusty taxi pulled up in front of the modest house her uncle had long ago given her. It was small but quaint. It was painted with brilliant colors--reds and greens and yellows and pinks. Loud. How appropriate, he thought. The house was set on a nice, grassed site with tall palm trees. Exotic fruit trees were scattered throughout the back and side yards. There was a perfect view of the ocean waves to the west. He could smell the salt air. No one else had known about the house. But he knew. He remembered. When the children were grown and she was finally alone her plan was to escape to this hideaway on the northern beaches of Costa Rico's Pacific coast. It was one of their many long-kept secrets.

Long straight rows of vibrant purple and pink and white tropical flowers blossomed along the front fence and down the narrow walkway. The air was thick with their sweet fragrance. "How do I love thee, let me count the ways," he remembered that famous poem. It looked like a nice, comfortable, happy place to live.

He stopped at the front door, sweating from the late afternoon heat, or maybe it was just from his being nervous. He gently knocked on the glass as anxious as a naughty school boy. After what seemed like an eternal few seconds the door opened.

She stood there looking into the sunlight, as gorgeous as he had remembered. In his mind he heard the *You're Beautiful...It's True* song. Her hair was different, streaked blond and short now, and she was still quite thin, almost

174

model-like. The years had favored her. Her face had a youthful glow. She was a vision. She was his life.

She hated surprises, but Brandon sensed that she had been waiting for him. Almost expecting him. Her beautiful face beamed and she smiled in delighted disbelief. It was the smile that he had envisioned every night for those so many years. The same wonderful welcoming smile that had drawn him from thousands of miles away and a life so long ago.

Her big dark eyes welled up with long held-back tears. A lifetime of anticipation had re-entered her world. The universe had allowed things to come full circle. Like it always did. As it was meant to be.

They looked at each other for the longest time without saying a word. He saw the square cut emerald ring on her finger that he had given to her for her birthday more than a decade ago. She was still wearing it after all this time. Well what do you know? He thought to himself with a gleam in his eyes. He felt good about it.

"Hello beautiful," he said to his lovely Angelina through a wide, exhilarating smile.

"Glad to see you, white boy," she finally spoke. Her walls were gone.

In the middle of the tropics surrounded by God's pure natural beauty touched by a warm coastal breeze, after all they had been through—the excitement, the sheer thrill of feeling wanted, the disappointments, the heartbreaks, the maturing of their inexplicable friendship—he had found his long lost friend, his love.

And she hers.

Brandon entered the small house, closed the door behind them, put his arms around Angelina's waist, held her tight, kissed her for the very first time and said, "DITTO.

Excerpt from author's book, *Sinless Guilt*

'I'm Okay'

Mom and Dad changed our lives when they took the bold step to move to the country. We left the dingy third floor apartment built in the early 1900s on Laurel Street in Somerville, Massachusetts. We moved to the country, to a small two bedroom, one bath cottage on a big open lot at 16 Dewey Avenue in Wilmington, north of the dirty city. It was 1955. It was a very good move.

Dad was a taxi driver working out of Cambridge. He put in long hours and had a long daily commute. He was the family bread winner and took his lot in life seriously. Mom stayed at home with her sons. It was the norm back then. She shopped and cooked and cleaned and took care of her children. I was six years old. My name is Bob. My brother Eddie had just turned five. Our new house was surrounded by dense woods, bordered by creeks and swamps, filled with adventure never imagined in the stark city. Eddie and I had discovered kid heaven.

A few years later Mom had another child in the spring of 1957. Another boy. His name was Stephen Michael Johnson. All of us boys had been given Christian middle names. At seven I didn't really understand why my new brother had to stay in the hospital for a long time. Mom came home and Dad missed a lot of work. Every day they went to the hospital to see Steve. It wasn't until sometime later I was told why.

My brother Steve had a rough time as a newborn. I guess it was touch and go for a while. Mom was strong and Dad stayed stoic. We didn't know if Steve would ever come home. Eddie and I just wondered silently what would happen to baby Steve. Kids weren't allowed to visit in hospitals so we had never seen our new brother. It was a scary time.

Weeks later Steve did come home. He was small and bundled and red, but he was home. Mom was happy. Dad went back to work. Eddie and I loved our brother. The doctors said he would gradually grow stronger and do well. They said he would be okay.

As kids we enjoyed living in the country. Silver Lake was about a half mile from our house. In the summer we spent most of our time there. We went swimming at the clean Town Beach and at the smaller private beaches around the lake. We floated in old tire tubes in the warm water under the lazy sun. We picnicked on the washed sands. We fished for perch and bluegill on the banks of the lake.

Steve loved to fish. When he was about four years old we walked down Main Street to our favorite fishing spot. It was off the rocky embankment across the street from the old Steven's Market. We would always catch small fish with our basic gear. I had a small red tackle box with line and plastic bobbers and leaded weights. Earlier in the day Steve and I dug for worms in our backyard near the septic tank. We stuffed plenty of big juicy earthworms into an empty Welch's jelly jar with holes poked in the top lid.

We'd spend hours fishing and killing worms and arguing and fussing. On good days we found some empty soda bottles on the way and traded them in at Tats, the corner store across from the lake. Penny candy was good, but ice cream cones were a treat. One day Steve slipped on the wet rocks and fell into the lake. It wasn't deep, but it wasn't a beach either. He had gone in, dunked up to his head.

I reached down and pulled him up onto the rocks. I remember yelling at him for dropping the rod and reel in the water too. "Are you alright?" I asked. I didn't want him to be hurt. I didn't want to get in trouble either for him getting hurt. He was crying. After all, he was a little kid. He was sopping wet from his sneakers to his blond hair. But he was a tough kid. He wiped the water from his face and said, "I'm okay." Then we went home with a bucket load of fish.

Years later I had my first car. It was a huge thrill as a sixteen year old to own a car. It was a 1958 Ford Fairland red-white two tone beauty. Except for its dented fender, rusted out front light panels, and rotted running boards. It got me to school and to work as a bag boy at DeMoulas, the local supermarket. It also got me to McDonald's. Back in the day there was only one McDonald's restaurant in the area. It was way over in North Reading, but any kid who had a car went there on the weekend.

We backed our rides into the parking spots around the small restaurant. Great classic cars were owned by the rich kids. Muscle cars. Corvettes, Mustangs, beautiful Chevy Nomads. And then guys like me had the rust buckets. But it was fun. It was the thing to do. Order your food and eat in your car, because at that time the fast food joint had no inside dining.

One weekend after I got paid I took my brother Steve for a burger. Big brother and little brother going out where the cool guys hung. Steve was excited. He had never been to a McDonald's. The only hamburgers he ever had were cooked at home. At the time it was highly unusual to go out to eat. People only ate out on special occasions, like birthdays and anniversaries.

I remember him looking out the windows as we drove. It was his first time in my car beyond the grocery store. The lot was filled with cool rides. Steve asked questions about the cars and the guys hanging around. He asked if McDonald's had milkshakes and if he could order one. Funny now, how such a simple trip could be so exhilarating.

We got our hamburgers and fries and thick milkshakes, all for not much more than a buck. We ate in the car, watching the people. Enjoying the moment. It was nice spending time with my little brother. I didn't do it often enough, probably because of the age difference. But it felt good. When it was time to go I asked Steve if he had had enough to eat. Then I asked matter-of-factly, "You good?"

He smiled. I think he enjoyed the trip and the time with his big brother more than the food. He sucked down the last of his strawberry shake and said, "I'm good. I'm okay."

In 1968 the Viet Nam War was going strong. Tens of thousands of young American teenagers were going to war. During my last years in high school many of my friends and I attended military funerals of students a year ahead of us. I signed up for the Air Force, a four year commitment. Steve was only ten. He knew where I was headed. He watched the TV news.

When I was ready to ship out to basic training I knew Steve was anxious. He was quiet and stayed to himself. I think he had a hard time dealing with me leaving the house. His entire life I had been around him. I tried to do things with my little brother, but knew it wasn't enough. He was a great kid and I didn't want him to worry. I had plenty to worry about myself.

I knew my younger brother Eddie would also sign up once he graduated. It was inevitable. Mom and Dad wouldn't be very thrilled having their two oldest boys in the military during such a dangerous time. But we do what we do. When it was time to go I went to Steve in the small living room in the house we had both grown up in. He was my little buddy. I felt for him.

"I'll be back," I told him.

My brother didn't say anything. He looked around me, not looking me in the eyes. He started to cry. It caused me to cry too. I hugged his skinny shoulders, trying to wipe my face dry.

"Everyone's leaving," he said, breathing heavy and gasping air. "You...and soon Eddie."

"We'll be fine, buddy. Besides, that makes you the man in charge." Months earlier Mom had another baby boy. He was named James, and being the youngest of four boys, he would be a handful. "It's gonna be your job to help Mom with Jimmy. You need to watch over him."

Steve nodded. He sniffled and used his hands to wipe his eyes and nose. He let a grin break loose.

"You gonna be okay?" I asked.

"Yeah, I'm okay."

During the next decade many things changed. I had a young family and we moved from Wilmington to Arizona. A man searching for his fortune. Shortly after, Steve came to the desert too. We worked and played together almost daily. It was a great time in my life. Steve was a hard worker. He was fun to be around. He was adventurous. He was a decent person. But in a secretive way I think he was filled with self-doubt. Too often the clown in the group, the comedian of the crowd is the one most unsure of himself.

When our Dad passed away at an early age his four boys were at his funeral. Bobby, Eddie, Steve, and Jimmy. The Johnson boys. He had given us a chance at a good life by taking us out of the city, by instilling in us the traits of honesty and consideration and commitment and a solid work ethic. You can't fake good kids, and Mom and Dad did a great job.

Losing our Dad was traumatic. He was the man in our life. He was our friend. He was our teacher, our mentor. And most definitely he was our hero who had done his best as a loving father. Being the eldest son I thought it would be appropriate if all Dad's sons went up to him lying in state to bid our farewell to a great man. A statement from his boys. It was a difficult time.

Steve couldn't handle the situation. He couldn't force himself to join us. He was too close to Dad since Eddie and I had moved on. He was too sensitive to accept the fact that his Dad had died. I completely understood his feelings. It's not easy losing someone so dear and near to you.

Steve pushed his way outside to the street. He lit a cigarette to calm his nerves and hung with other friends who came to give their respects. Jimmy joined him too. Then Eddie and me. It was cold outside and the leaves had fallen from the trees. As one, we four brothers hugged. Dad knew we were there.

I patted Steve on the back. "How you holding up brother?" I asked, although I already knew what he would say.

"I'm okay, Bob. I'm okay."

I knew he wasn't okay. Not really. But there was nothing I could do. People are what they are. I admired him for being him. I understood how he felt. I appreciated his honesty, his sincere grieving. I loved my brother, but I had to return home to my family and my work and my life. I hoped in time Steve could accept what had happened.

2001 was not a good year for our nation, or for our family. Mom passed away after a lengthy illness and complications due to her leukemia. Brother Jimmy had been living with her in a small, rundown apartment. They were a pair of lovable characters. They were buds. They were happy with each other and depended on each other. I got the chance to visit them before the end.

The Johnson boys went through the same motions as when Dad had died. A big funeral, with lots of family and friends gathered in those final sad moments. A person doesn't often realize what a positive impact others have made when a loved one passes. I saw the tremendous outpouring of love for our Mom. People from far and near came. They told stories I had never heard. They remembered grand events. They shared photos of good times. They laughed at the funny things and cried for the moment. It reminded me how fortunate my brothers and I were.

We said goodbye to our mother. We had sixty-nine years of her love and in her absence was a huge gaping hole. Jimmy and Steve were strong. They stayed quiet in their own thoughts, probably wondering how such a thing could happen. Our brother Eddie was not there. He had disappeared some twelve years earlier. Simply disappeared off the face of the earth. He had no idea what happened to Mom. And we had no idea of what happened to him. It was a very long time until we found out.

Boston winters can be brutal. Cold and raw, wet and miserable. Right before Christmas of 2016 I called Steve to wish him a Merry Christmas. I didn't call him often enough, which I should have. I knew he lived a tough life. Hard outside construction work pouring concrete. It was a younger man's job. Unsteady paychecks. Wicked winters. But he was a typical tough New Englander. Nose to the grindstone. Do the best you can. Don't complain. Just live with what you've got. Something good is to be said of that lifestyle. Something commendable.

Fortunately, Steve had someone wonderful in his life. His wife Ruthie was good to him. She was good for him. They shared life together. They did things together. They liked being together. They were happy even when things didn't go right. Ruthie was Steve's sweet princess. I had met her only a couple times. Only at funerals. Why do we do that? She is a good, decent person and I was glad she was with my brother.

Steve had somehow acquired the nickname of 'Stunch.' Back home it seemed everyone had a given nickname. I don't know where that came from or who gave it to him, but I always thought it humorous. It brought a smile to my face whenever I heard it. Not being around him much I never felt right calling him Stunch. I'm old school. I always did and always will call him Steve.

When I spoke to Steve long distance on that cold December day I was surprised. "How've you been brother?" I asked, expecting him to answer that everything was fine despite the weather.

"I'm okay," he said in his typical don't-worry-about-me tone.

I knew he had COPD, chronic obstructive pulmonary disease, which prevented him from breathing normally. His breathing was labored and difficult. His lungs had partially shut down. Because of his disease he couldn't work. It was like a prison sentence to him. He liked to work. He had to work. Work defined him. But with the irreversible disease he had to accept the diagnosis and situation.

Steve continued his conversation on the phone. "Our apartment burned down," he said casually.

"Oh no! How'd that happen?"

"They said it was electrical. We still have a few things from storage. But we're okay."

"So where are you staying?" I had to know.

"In our van. It's broke down but we have blankets and our dog. It's warm enough."

"It's nineteen degrees there!" I yelled into the phone. That wasn't right.

"We'll be okay," my brother said, pushing his problems away.

"Can you stay somewhere? How about a motel or something?"

"Yeah, well, I've been out of work for a while. Don't worry about us Bob. We'll be okay."

I was stunned. My brother and Ruthie and their dog were burned out of their home. They were living in a freezing broken down van. Steve had no income because of his lung disease. All of this was happening and all he would say was, "We're okay."

"Do something about it Steve," I said.

"Okay Bob. Thanks for calling. I have to go now. I'll call you later." And that's all he said.

I knew he wouldn't call. He was too proud, too stubborn to ask for help. Of course I felt terrible. My brother was in a real bad spot. I was three thousand miles away. I had to do something. I'm not a rich man but I could help some. People are what they are. People do what they do. I hung up the silent phone wishing I had been a better big brother.

Within the year Steve had been in and out of the hospital for his disease. They found a new place to move into. Oddly enough it was a stone's throw from where we had grown up on 16 Dewey Ave. People say life is a giant circle with a beginning and an end. We had no idea it was set in play with my brother Steve.

After many tests and many doctors' appointments and many consultations Steve was admitted to Tufts Medical Center in Boston, one of the top hospitals around. Surgery was performed on Steve's cancerous lung. Then the waiting began. Stuck in a hospital bed with tubes stuck in him and monitors strapped to him, Steve was restless. He wanted to go home. He wanted to play with his dog. He wanted to go fishing. He wanted to be with Ruthie. He just wanted to have a normal life.

Over the next months he showed improvement, then his condition worsened. I called him and of course he said he would be okay. Ruthie drove the hour trip every day to his hospital bed. She was his angel. She cared for him and made his long days tolerable. She remained strong and optimistic. She wanted the man she loved home too. But she was rightfully concerned.

Near the end when Steve's body gave in to the disease and infections and attacks and medication, I believe he knew Ruthie was beside him. I asked her if he was responsive. She said no, but he would press her hand ever so slightly while she held his.

I think he knew the end was near. I think he felt loved. I think he was ready to go. I think by gently squeezing his fingers against the lady he loved he was saying, 'Don't worry about me. I'm okay.'

Last Day in Paradise

It was another ideal spring day in the life of Harold K. Landerson. From his open bedroom window he could feel the sun warming up the morning air. It was clean and light and refreshing. He smelled the sweet wildflowers in the pasture beyond the trees and heard the sparrows chirping their songs. It was a perfect day for the eighty-nine year old man.

And it was almost his last.

A day earlier Harold had a doctor's appointment. He drove there himself, although his driver's license had expired two years earlier. He would never have passed the eye test so he simply continued to drive. The specialists reviewed Harold's thick medical file. There were lots of reports and test results and consultation remarks in the folder. Old X-rays and medication prescriptions and heart surgery details rounded out the file.

Harold was not a healthy man. His doctors knew it. He knew it too. His heart was giving out. Had been for the past several years. The wear and tear of nine decades had taken its toll. End stage congestive heart failure was the official diagnosis by a team of specialists. Before leaving the hospital and his regimen of doctors, Harold was told nothing could be done for him. No procedure. No surgery. No treatment. No new miracle drug. In other words the blunt answer was the end was very near.

"How much time do I have?" Harold asked his primary physician with no hint of worry.

"Not long I'm afraid," the doctor said. "Could be a week, a couple days, maybe less."

The old man just looked at him. "Thanks doc," he said. Then he turned to leave.

Harold had been sent home, instructed to continue taking his medication. He was told to rest and drink plenty of fluids. He was told to put his affairs in order and be with his family.

Harold drove home very slowly. He pushed the buttons and lowered all the windows in his car. The fresh air whipped through. It felt good on his face and blew through what little hair he had left. He waved at a few people crossing the road. He watched children kicking a ball in the park. He stared at the white clouds floating away.

He wasn't afraid to die. He was ready. Well, almost. He had no regrets for what he had done in his long life. He had no regrets for what he hadn't done either. Well, perhaps there were a few. All was well, though. He'd lived a good life and by golly he was going to make the most of his last day on earth if that was all he had.

Holding onto the stoop railing as he stepped unsteadily into his home, Harold saw his wife in the kitchen. He smiled at the woman he had been married to for nearly sixty-seven years. She turned from the stove and saw her dear husband. Silvia was still a beautiful lady in his eyes. Of course at eighty-six her hair was gray and her face showed wrinkles, but she was still a stunning woman.

"Good, you're home," Silvia said. "I made us lunch."

At the kitchen table as they ate their soup and toast Silvia knew something was wrong. She knew her husband perfectly. He was quiet but seemed content. She waited for him to speak first.

"There's nothing they can do," Harold said, referring to his doctor's diagnosis. His voice wasn't excited. No sadness came through. It simply was what it was.

Silvia slipped her thin hand into his. Almost seventy years together and she loved this man even more than before. More now than when they had first fallen in love. More than the day they were married. Time refines love, reveals its true depth. They finished their lunch together without speaking another word.

Harold sat in his favorite worn chair in the living room. His books were neatly lined up in the large bookcase. The classics. Books of history. Travel books. Pictures of the kids and grandkids hung on the walls. An ancient phonograph, once new to them, sat in the corner with a stack of old records on the bottom shelf. It was a comfortable room.

He wondered what most people would do if they knew the exact day they were going to die. Would they feel depressed and roll up and die? Would they fight the inevitable, praying for more time? Would they complain and regret those things that never happened? Would they seize their final moments in grief?

No. Harold would do none of those. Life was good and death was part of it. A new chapter, if one believed. He had lived a spectacular life. He had wonderful children who turned out to be great human beings. He had fantastic grandchildren and great-grandchildren who had promising lives ahead of them. He had good friends, some of whom he had known since childhood. He had few complaints.

He rested comfortably in his chair. Did he get everything he ever wanted in life? No, but he understood that rarely happened. However, there was no doubt he had everything he needed. Did all his dreams and ambitions come true? No, but they didn't really matter. He had done his best and that was all anyone could hope for. And he never quit. He never gave up on himself or the people he loved.

A long time ago Harold had decided to squeeze out every precious minute of his life. He would enjoy life despite its drawbacks. He would overcome obstacles no matter how big. He would embrace each and every day. He had figured out that 'one' thing in life. He had discovered the real meaning of life and love, and that's how he wanted to go out.

Tomorrow could likely be his last day on this earth, he figured. He was committed not to waste one minute of it. Life was a gift and he would thoroughly enjoy it even to the very end.

The next morning Harold woke up at 6:10, much earlier than usual. He had a full day ahead of him. He got dressed and went for a short walk along his regular route through the neighborhood. It was another sunny, but cool morning. He could smell the newness of spring. People were driving to work. School kids were running to their buses. Some joggers paced themselves in their daily rituals. Other walkers went their own way to places unknown. Life was all around him.

Back home Silvia made him a full breakfast. The smells filled the house. Crispy bacon, hash browns, scrambled eggs with cheese, buttered toast, coffee with sugar and cream. Ahhh! It tasted sinfully good and was worth every bite. After all, it couldn't hurt him now.

"Thank you dear," Harold said to his wife. "Later let me take you somewhere for lunch."

After the breakfast dishes were cleaned both Harold and Silvia sat on the couch. Silvia pulled several filled photo albums from the shelves. They slowly turned the pages of their lives together. Their first date back in the late 1940s. Harold was so nervous he had forgotten his wallet. Silvia ended up paying. Their first house, a tiny bungalow in the city with the one bathroom next to the kitchen pantry. Pictures of their newborn children, the best days in their lives. First, Benjamin, their son. Then two years later their daughter Melissa. The vacations they took as a family. The beaches and boating and skiing and hiking and airplane trips. Anniversaries and birthday parties and graduation celebrations. Different jobs in different cities. New cars and new grandchildren.

These were the important things in life. These were what made life worth living. The snapshots of their lives. The memories that last forever. Even beyond forever.

Later in the morning Harold called his son. "Are you okay, Dad?" Benjamin asked. He could hear telling things in his dad's voice. His son was worried, but he knew too.

Harold said to his boy, "I'm fine. Just wanted to talk to you for a while."

And they talked for a long while. About Ben's little league games when he was a young boy. When they went to see the Red Sox at Fenway Park. The times he got in trouble. When he got hurt falling from a tree. His old friends. His new job.

Then Harold called his daughter. She lived nearby and stopped by the house at least once a week to see her aging parents. Daughters tend to do that more than sons. Melissa was a lot like her father. She was ambitious, liked to stay busy, liked to travel, liked adventure. She and her dad spoke for some time and promised to see each other soon.

Before noon Harold walked around his house. He sat in the kitchen for a bit, then in the living room, sucking in the smells and sights and memories held close by the familiar walls. From his desk in the den he found his life insurance policy folder and placed it on the desk. He wanted to make things easier for Silvia when the time came.

By 12:30 the Landersons went out for lunch at their favorite restaurant. It was a small place hidden in a side street where they used to go on special occasions. Harold would bring Silvia there on Valentine's Day and surprise her with a bouquet of red roses. On more than one birthday Harold would give his wife a piece of jewelry. A pair of diamond ear rings. A silver bracelet. A nice watch. Sometimes they went there just to have coffee and a slice of apple pie.

They ate a light salad and some grilled salmon with wine. It felt like their first date. They smiled and laughed and told stories and reminisced. They both enjoyed the time, but their eyes revealed what was really happening.

Back at home Harold took a nap on the couch. It wasn't unusual for him to rest there each afternoon. After a short nap he always felt renewed.

By 6:00 that evening Silvia had cooked up some spicy Italian sausage and baked beans. It was Harold's favorite meal of all. His needs were simple. It reminded him of when he was a kid back in the streets of Boston.

Later when it turned dark outside, the couple spent some time on their front porch. They sat and gently swayed in the swing seat. It was a nice evening. A chill had formed in the light breeze. The smell of honeysuckle floated in the air. They took a slow walk through their yard. The moonlight reflected off the patio Harold had built and the garden Silvia had tended.

Then inside they watched their anniversary video together. The one when Harold had surprised his wife by scheduling a huge marriage renewal vow celebration in their back yard. That was almost thirty years ago. Harold went to the freezer and put a small scoop of vanilla ice cream into two cups, one for him and one for Silvia like he had done most every evening. While watching the video they barely spoke. Harold hugged his wife and Silvia hugged her husband.

By 10:00 they went to bed, Harold walking behind his loving wife down the hallway, their hands entwined. He was tired but felt excited, as if it was his first time with young Silvia back in the day. They dressed in their pajamas and got into their big old comfortable bed.

Lying under the warm covers Harold wrapped his arm around his wife. It felt nice. It felt right. They had spent a third of their lives together in this room. Warm and soft. Comfortable and safe. Satisfying and reassuring.

He didn't say anything. He didn't want to leave her. He softly kissed Silvia on her cheek. Her warm tears rolled down her cheeks onto his chest. It made him cry too. He held her tighter, not wanting to ever let go. He just looked up at the dark ceiling, the fan gently moving the bedroom air. He loved this woman.

They lay in bed together, the same bed they had made love in a thousand times, the same bed they had never gone to sleep angry at each other. The same bed they had dreamed in and made life plans in and rested in.

"I'm sorry Silvia," Harold whispered. He felt weak and almost out of breath.

"Sorry? Sorry for what?" she asked, tears still in her most beautiful eyes.

"You know."

"What? Harold! What are you sorry about?"

"I'm sorry I let you down."

"What are you saying? How in the world have you let me down?" she asked. She bent over and looked at him.

"All my promises to you. Everything I've ever wanted to give you. Everything I couldn't give to you. I'm sorry for not giving you a better life. I'm sorry for being a failure." He turned his head on the pillow away from his wife so she couldn't see his eyes misting up with decades of secret regret and years of self-doubt..

"I'm sorry for it all."

Silvia looked at her dying husband. "Harold. You have given me more than I could ever imagine. I have never been without. I have never been disappointed. I have loved you since the moment we met and I will always love you. You...Harold...have made my life wonderful."

Harold forced a smile. He coughed and tried to gulp down a deep breath. "I love you too, my Silvia,"

Then Harold laid his head on his pillow and closed his eyes. He moved his hand to his wife's. It was like finishing a good book that he didn't want to end. But it was the end and it had been an excellent story of a good man's last day in paradise.

Made in the USA
Monee, IL
19 November 2024

70537696R00108